THE
LEGEND
OF
SINGLE
CLAW

THE LEGEND OF SINGLE CLAW

STAN WING

XULON PRESS

Xulon Press
555 Winderley Pl, Suite 225
Maitland, FL 32751
407.339.4217
www.xulonpress.com

xulon
PRESS

Paperback ISBN-13: 979-8-86850-542-3
Ebook ISBN-13: 979-8-86850-543-0

TABLE OF CONTENTS

INTRODUCTION

It's been fifty years since I started telling stories about a bear called Single claw. I can't recall all the joy and adventure that the old bear has given me. You're probably wondering, what's this all about. Why did I decide to write a book about a bear? Well, it's not a book about a bear. He's just got one of the leading roles. It's a book about building a bond and connecting with your children and grandchildren. The stories I wrote down were originally oral stories, like the ones that were told before the world of A.I.,TV, DVD;s and all the other technology.

Here's how it evolved. In the evening after supper I would often tell stories to my children. Sometimes under a sheet draped over a table simulating a tent and campout. We had no TV reception and haven't had for the past fifty years. I believe TV can be one of the greatest time robbers of imagination ever made. I had a desire to build bonds with my children with oral storytelling like was common for my grandparents when they were children. I picture the pioneers sitting around a campfire with covered wagons in the background and captivated little children clinging to every spoken word. It was a perfect way to show your children you care enough about them to spend time with them.

The side plot of my stories hinges around a bear that had all his claws on his right paw burnt off except one. Hence the name Single Claw. This cub grew up to be the largest and meanest grizzly in the world. Now every time it comes across a campfire, something that would normally ward off animals, it goes into a murderous rage attacking the fire and anyone around it.

This leads us to the main theme of these stories. My children and grand kids. I never imagined how much the children would love the controlled suspense and danger they would be involved with. The children became the main characters in the stories. They would be the one's saving lives and protecting others from this dangerous bear called 'Single Claw.' They would become the real hero's.

I always recommend that readers change the names of my grandkids to their own if they can. You can see the response in their eyes when their name is mentioned. It draws them into the story like bee's to honey.

I remember one Sunday evening with my grandkids when it was time for another weekly story about Single Claw. They told their visiting friend, it was time for another bear story. She didn't want to go. She thought it was dumb I guess. They brought her over anyway and she complained to me that she didn't want to hear it.

"But, Ashlyn I said," you're in the story.

"No I'm not." she said. "How could that be?"

"Oh but you are." As I planned to replace one of my kids' names occasionally with hers.

"Alright, how did they spell it?"

Not being known for my spelling genius, I thought 'here goes nothing.'

"ASHLYN." She looked surprised and said, "Well, somebody finally got it right." She enjoyed being in the story and became a convert of Single Claw, wanting to come for more.

One thing I've observed is, to my surprise, adults enjoy these stories equally as well as the children. I'm often asked, "Do you have more?"

Some have asked, why don't you have any illustrations? The reason I don't is, they were originally oral stories. I didn't have the talent to draw them myself or see the need. I've learned that their own imagination is far more creative than I thought. They are there in living color in their own mind. Each one creates how they see it.

"One evening toward the end of a story, the grandkids had just saved the lives of a famous wealthy fisherman and his son from Single Claw. As they were coming back to town they saw a banner across the street welcoming and congratulating them. The newspaper and TV cameras were there to take their picture. All of a sudden, my granddaughter Jessie interrupted and began waving her hand.

"Grandpa, Grandpa," she called.

"What is it Jessie?"

"Do I have long hair or short hair," she asked.

Once again, I had to take a guess. "Ah, you have long hair."

"Oh good," she said, "I look better with long hair."

It told me how real in their minds, they are in these stories.

Another small benefit of no illustrations is, they don't jump up and run around me to see what the illustration is at every turn of the page. When reading these stories to your children, learn to show excitement, fear, joy and calmness. In other words, show emotion. Learn to growl like a bear when Single Claw is closing in on you.

I try to interject Godly, moral values into my stories like the golden rule, what's right and wrong, good and evil and just plain living for the Lord Jesus Christ by following His commands. Strong family ties are encouraged with the grandkids in the stories spending time with their grandparents as they take on one exciting adventure after another.

These stories take place in a fictitious place in the far north called Sawdust Springs where the children spend their summers with their grandparents. You'll get to know characters like sheriff Perkins, Rawhide Jake, Cactus Calhoon, places like Loon Lake, Bear Mountain, the Caribou River and the Sawdust Springs Ranger Station.

Now, all but three of our twelve grandchildren have grown into adulthood. My wife and four children, who are soon getting to retirement age, kept saying, "You need to write some of your stories down for posterity." So finally I wrote five of my short stories to make up one book. Believe me, it's a lot harder to write one than to tell one!

I hope this gives you a taste of what and why I'm doing with the 'Legend of Single Claw.' Time is racing past with breakneck speed. Before you know it, our children are grown up and on their own. The window of time we have with them is narrow. Somewhere between the ages of six and twelve seems to be the prime time for their interest in these stories, but this varies with each child. That's not very long. I encourage you to spend quality time with your children. It's what the Lord wants!

STORY ONE

SECRET TREASURE OF BEAR MOUNTAIN

Our story begins with an event that took place many years ago at the close of the Civil War. The year was 1865.

The crimson glow of fire set the night sky ablaze as southern cities burned to the ground. After four long years, the Civil war was finally coming to an end. The thunder of cannons could be heard in the distance and the smell of smoke and gun powder filled the air as the Union army advanced without restraint, leaving a swath of destruction in its path.

Twenty miles from the city of Atlanta in a remote farmhouse, President Jefferson Davis, dressed in full military uniform, paced nervously back and forth on the creaky wooden floor. He was about to give his last orders as president of the confederate states to a band of rebel soldiers.

"Faithful Soldiers of the confederate," spoke the president in a somber voice, "our darkest hour is before us. The war will soon be lost. Because of your bravery and loyalty, you've been chosen for the most important mission of your life. What I'm asking you to do tonight will sustain our resolve to live in a free and independent republic. The hope of rebuilding our great nation rests upon your shoulders. Our very survival is entrusted to your success."

After final instructions about their secret mission, twelve heavy wagons loaded with a valuable, precious cargo, quietly slipped away into the darkness just ahead of the Union Army. They were carrying with them boxes of hope. Hope that someday the south will rise again. It will be over a hundred years later before the content of those boxes is revealed.

CHAPTER 1

THE SEARCH PARTY

I n the far north, beneath majestic Bear Mountain, lies a little logging town called Sawdust Springs. This quiet, peaceful community is soon to discover the truth of a mysterious Indian legend about a giant bear called Single Claw.

Sheriff Perkins has just called a town meeting of all the able-bodied men to meet in front of Holly's General Store. The restless crowd grew impatient as they waited for the Sheriff to arrive. Finally, he walked through the curious group of men and stepped up onto the wooden boardwalk. A hush grew over the crowd and all eyes focused on the tall man wearing the star.

"Men, the reason I've called all of you here today is to help one of our old prospectors, Rawhide Jake. He's been our friend for as long as I can remember. As you know, Rawhide comes into town every year just after the spring thaw to get supplies. It's been three weeks now since the thaw, and no one's seen hide nor hair of him. What I need is a search party with two volunteers to see if anything's happened to the old timer. I'd go myself, but I have to take a prisoner back to Pleasantville."

"But sheriff," whined Skeeter Jones, "you know nobody knows the whereabouts of Rawhide's cabin. Not that we haven't wanted to find it, but every time someone tries to follow him back to his cabin, he just seems to disappear back into those mountains. We suspect he's got a gold mine somewhere up on Bear Mountain because that's all he ever pays with, large gold nuggets. We'd like nothing better than to know the location of that mine, but every time we try to follow him,he gives us the slip."

"I know men, but we still have to try. After all, I'd do the same for any of you if I thought you were in trouble. All I need is two volunteers."

"Aren't you forgetting something, Sheriff?" asked Ralph Jordan, the town's undertaker. "The legend of Single Claw. That's one reason a lot of us don't care to venture to the back side of Bear Mountain. How Rawhide survives with that bear is a mystery to us. Maybe his luck just ran out."

"Why, Single Claw's just a bunch of superstition," responded Sheriff Perkins. "You don't really believe that old Indian legend, do you?"

"It's true all right! All eyes turned to Scar-face Sam as he walked up to the back of the crowd. He stood there looking like something out of a nightmare with one hand raised in the air and the other pointing to his disfigured face. His horrific features were hard to look at.

"It was Single Claw who did this to me some twelve years ago. I was the lucky one they say. The only one out of six men to survive his attack that dark December night

4

as we sat around the campfire. Yeah, he's real all right, as sure as the grave waits for us all, he's real. You better take heed to this, *anyone who goes to the backside of Bear Mountain will never come back alive!* Don't say you haven't been warned about that killer bear."

With that, the crowd grew silent and nervous, and some began to leave. Sheriff Perkins knew he had to do something and do it fast.

"Now wait a minute men, hold on there. I know some of you have doubts about going to Bear Mountain, but that still doesn't change the fact that the old timer is missing. We don't want to let fear stop us from doing what's right, do we? I'm offering to pay all expenses and give a $100 reward to whoever finds our old friend, Rawhide Jake".

With that, Clem Johnson and Jed Baker stepped forward. "We'll go sheriff," hollered Clem. "We're not afraid of whatever is out there on Bear Mountain. Besides, we could sure use the money right now. Work has been pretty scarce around here this winter."

"Money won't do you any good when you're dead," hollered Scar-face Sam. "Single Claw doesn't care how much money you're making."

"Now you be quiet," shouted back Sheriff Perkins. "I'll take full responsibility for their safety."

Across town at the train station, two anxious grandparents waited for the arrival of their grandkids from the big city. Every year, Aria, Taven and Maddox came to

Sawdust Springs for a summer filled with fun and adventure. They loved to hike, fish, camp and help out around the ranch. But the best part was having their own horses to ride the trails around Bear Mountain. It was a kid's paradise. For the next three months they would exchange city life for the rugged and beautiful wilderness of the far north.

Finally, the train pulled into Sawdust Springs and Three excited travelers ran out onto the wooden platform. They shouted with joy when they saw their grandparents. After the happy reunion with hugs and laughter, they gathered their bags and headed to the log cabin at the edge of town. They could hardly wait to see the ranch again. The log cabin, barn, stockyard, chicken coop and horse corral with their own horses waiting to be smothered with affection. The smell of leather, horses, hay and home cooking brought back wonderful memories. Back in the city, they were just one of the crowd, but here at Sawdust Springs they were treated like extra- special royalty. To them, the only thing better than this would be Heaven itself.

After unpacking and washing up, everyone gathered in the kitchen for one of Grandma's famous home cooked meals prepared over a wood fired cook stove.

During supper, Aria was the first to ask Grandpa what they were going to do this summer. (She was the oldest, Maddox the youngest, with Taven in the middle.)

"Well, I don't rightly know. What would you like to do?" answered Grandpa. "We could go fishing, hiking, riding horses, camping or maybe we could just go looking for Rawhide Jake?"

"What?" said Taven and Maddox at the same time.

"Yeah," Joined in Aria, what do you mean, 'look for Rawhide Jake'?"

Grandpa explained the situation and then told about the $100 reward Sheriff Perkins had offered.

"$100 dollars," Gasped Aria. "That's it, "adventure, mystery, and reward all wrapped up into one!"

The others agreed, this would be a great way to start off the summer.

"My only concern," said Grandpa, "is the talk around town about a bear they call Single Claw. Some think it's too dangerous to go to the back side of Bear Mountain where he's supposed to live. Especially after two fishermen disappeared this spring while fishing the headwaters of the Caribou River."

"But I thought all those rumors about a gigantic bear were just the results of someone's imagination, weren't they Grandpa?" asked Taven.

Well, that's what I've always thought, but maybe there is something to it. Scar-face Sam sure believes he's real."

"Oh, please, begged the children, "we'll be safe. Let's go to Loon Lake and stay at the Sawdust Springs Ranger Station. We've gone there every summer and we've never; ever seen a dangerous bear."

"Well, I suppose," said Grandpa, "We'll just have to be extra careful."

Maddox, let out his usual 'Jumping Horny toads,' we're going on another great adventure!

"If we're going to look for Rawhide, let's leave tomorrow as soon as we get all our gear packed." Instructed Grandpa. "I think we'd be better off going on foot and leaving the horses at home for this trip. That way we can keep a closer look out for tracks and clues."

The children had planned to hit the hay right after supper, but Grandpa began telling stories of the good old days when they first came to Sawdust Springs and started a homestead in the far north. It got later than Grandpa had planned but he knew that at special times like this, sharing your life story was much more important than a little sleep. Besides, the children loved hearing those stories about how God helped them out time and again during those tough years. It strengthened their faith and gave them a sense of security and belonging.

———————))⟨⟩((———————

Clem and Jed, the volunteers for Sheriff Perkins had been on the trail, looking for Rawhide Jake, for three days now, before the grand kids arrived in town. The sun was starting to go down and they were looking for a good place to make camp.

"There's a level spot up ahead," said Clem. "Looks like a perfect place to set up the tent." By the time they made camp and had supper it was pitch black. Sitting around the fire, they began making plans for the next day.

"I hope we have more luck tomorrow than we've had these last three days," said Jed. "We haven't found hide nor hair of any tracks, nowhere."

"I know," said Clem, "We've haven't seen anything, but I think something's seen us. I've had the strangest feeling that we're being watched."

"Me too," said Jed. "Didn't want to mention it before, but I've had the same feeling, like we're being followed ever since we got to the back side of Bear Mountain."

"Say," said Jed, "being new to these here parts, what was all that talk about a bear the other day. What were the people all riled up about anyway? What was it they called him, 'Single Paw?'

''No," said Clem, 'Single Claw!'" Reaching down and stoking the fire, he began telling the story. "It's just an old Indian legend. It goes like this. Supposedly, at one time, there was a forest fire on the backside of Bear Mountain. No one's ever seen evidence of a forest fire and that's one reason a lot of people don't believe it's true. Anyway, during the fire a small grizzly cub climbed a tree to escape the heat. It didn't do him much good though and he got burnt pretty bad. The fire burned off all the claws on his right paw except one. That's why they call him 'Single Claw.'

"What's so scary about that?" asked Jed.

"Now, just hold on," said Clem, "I haven't gotten to the scary part. Where was I? Oh yeah, well, that bear saved his life by jumping down from that tree and running into the cool waters of Wolf Creek. All that adrenaline and excitement caused something to happen to that little cub that made him keep growing. The old prospectors say he's the largest bear they've ever seen. But the worst part is, now, every time he sees a campfire, it reminds him of that terrible forest fire that burned him so bad, and he goes into a murderous rage, attacking anyone in sight and destroying the campfire."

"Do you believe that story?" asked Jed.

"Well I don't know, but one thing I do know is, the Indians sure believe it. You'll never find one of them here on the back side of Bear Mountain."

"Well then, what in the world are we doing here, sitting around a campfire on the backside of Bear Mountain?" questioned Jed.

Clem was about to answer when he heard what sounded like a low growl out in the darkness. They both froze with fear as they looked in the direction of the mysterious noise. Their eyes strained in the darkness looking for any movement.

"That's strange," whispered Jed, "look at those branches slowly moving." He paused for a moment with wide eyes as it dawned on him that there wasn't a breath of wind. Then a twig snapped as something started coming towards them.

"Who's there?" hollered Clem. Everything became quiet for several minutes. Whatever was out there in the darkness had stopped moving. The silence put their nerves on edge. The tension mounted and then another twig snapped. "What do you want?" yelled Jed, "come out and show yourself."

The tree branches began to sway again from something large coming closer to their camp. They could hear a low growl coming from the darkness.

Clem was shaking with fear as he slowly reached for his rifle. All of a sudden, it appeared. Something huge, silhouetted in the moonlight, stepped into the clearing. Two large, red eyes, at least fifteen feet from the ground, were staring at them.

" Wha, what's tha, tha, that?" stuttered Jed.

Just then a deafening roar came from the huge beast. The forest shook from the noise. For a few seconds they were paralyzed with fear, unable to move. Then Clem overcame his fear and shouted, "run, run for your life!"

They both took off into the darkness running as fast as they could, tripping and falling over brush and rocks. The huge monster charged after them and was quickly closing the gap. Closer and closer it came. A feeling of hopelessness swept over them as they could feel its breath on the back of their necks. Then something happened that they couldn't comprehend for a few seconds. They were falling. There was no ground underneath them, but their feet were still running. They had fallen off a steep cliff.

Before the fear of their new danger was realized, they plunged into the deep river far below. Coming to the surface, they managed to cling to a large log that was drifting by. Looking up to the ledge far above the river, they could see the silhouette of a giant bear swaying back and forth in the moonlight, snapping it's teeth and roaring with rage as he watched them drift away.

"What was that?" cried Jed. "Was that Single Claw?"

"I don't know," answered Clem, "but it definitely was the largest bear I've ever seen."

They held onto the log and drifted further and further down river, away from their worst nightmare.

"If I'm right," said Clem, "we've landed in the Caribou River that flows right through Sawdust Springs. Let's float downriver until it's safe and then pull ashore. We can build a makeshift raft in the morning. If all goes well, we should be able to drift back into town by late afternoon."

CHAPTER 2

The Hidden Trail

"Alright, men," shouted Sheriff Perkins, "the reason I've called another town meeting is to let you know what's happening in the search for Rawhide Jake. My volunteers, Clem and Jed, haven't been seen or heard from for five days now. They were supposed to make contact with me yesterday."

"What'd I tell you?" sneered Scarface Sam. "I told you anyone going to the backside of Bear Mountain would never come back alive."

"I know," said Sheriff Perkins, "but we don't know if they're in trouble or not. All I'd like is one more volunteer to go with me so I can find out what's happening out there on Bear Mountain. First, Rawhide Jake doesn't show up and now Jed and Clem aren't back when they're supposed to." He looked sternly at the crowd. "If nobody wants to volunteer, I'll go by myself."

After a few quiet moments, Doc Barns raised his hand. "I'll go, Sheriff, you might need the help of a medical doctor when we find those missing men."

"Thanks, Doc." Sheriff Perkins breathed a sigh of relief. "Before we go, let's post a sign at the outskirts of town warning people to stay away from Bear Mountain. We don't need anyone else lost out there while we're figuring this thing out. First we need to find Jed, Clem and Rawhide Jake."

--------------⟩⟨⟨⟩⟩⟨--------------

The next day, Grandpa and his Grandkids got their gear packed and headed out right after lunch. Their goal was to make it to the Sawdust Springs Ranger Station at Loon Lake before dark.

A beautiful sunset was reflecting on Loon lake by the time they arrived to set up camp. The Sawdust Springs Ranger Station was the only building left at the lake. It had long been abandoned after the gold rush. With its thick logs and wood stove to heat with, it made a perfect overnight shelter. They could hear the peaceful, haunting sounds of loons calling across the still, glass like waters as they spread out their sleeping bags. "You sure don't hear the call of loons back in the city where we live," commented Aria.

"Yeah," chimed in Taven, "this sure beats the sounds of traffic and sirens."

Grandpa agreed and reminded them that it was one of the reasons why he and Grandma liked to live in the far north. "I never tire of hearing the loons," said Grandpa. "There's nothing more relaxing than turning in after a busy day and listening to the untamed sounds of the northern wilderness."

"Speaking of turning in, we'd better keep moving. Maddox, you and Taven start the campfire while Aria helps me set up the cabin."

It wasn't long before baked beans, hot dogs and S'mores seasoned with the sights, sounds, and smells of the northern wilderness printed indelible memories on the hearts of our young campers. Sleep came easy as the loons sang their lullaby and a lone wolf howled in the distance.

Grandpa was the first to get up the next morning and start the fire. He decided to fix them their favorite breakfast, 'Bannock,' sometimes called 'Indian flat bread.'

After breakfast, Aria asked, "How much further up the trail are we going today?"

"Well, this is probably as far as we should go. I told your grandma we probably wouldn't go to the backside of the mountain with all that talk about Single Claw."

"Oh Grandpa," sighed Aria, "can't we go just a little further and look for tracks? We'll be OK with you."

"Well, I suppose we can go just a little further," conceded Grandpa. The children let out a squeal of delight.

"But you must stay close together and not venture off alone."

"It's a deal!" shouted the children.

After breaking camp, they headed further north on the trail that leads to the backside of Bear Mountain. The trail became steep and the going was rough. They'd covered about two miles when Maddox panted with deep breath, "Can we take a little break? my legs are killing me."

"Mine too," said Taven.

"OK troop," said Grandpa, "let's stop here and rest awhile. Besides, we should probably turn around and head back down the trail. I think we've gone far enough."

While sitting on a large log that was laying just off the trail, Grandpa broke out the Trail Mix and water.

"I'm surprised how good just plain water tastes when you're thirsty," said Aria. It never tastes this good at home." Just then, something caught Aria's eye. "Look guys, over there on the other side of this log."

"What is it?" asked Taven.

" I don't know. It looks like an old trail that someone tried to hide with a pile of branches."

"You're right Aria," said Grandpa. "Now, why would anyone go to all the trouble to hide a trail like that? If we hadn't stopped in this exact spot to take a break, we never would have seen it."

"Can we see where it goes?" asked Maddox. "Please?"

Grandpa was as curious as they were but tried not to let on. "I don't know, we probably should be turning back."

"Oh please," begged the children, "we're not tired anymore. Can we take a vote?"

"I suppose", said Grandpa, knowing how the vote would turn out.

"All in favor of exploring the hidden trail, raise your right hand." Quicker than a chicken jumping on a June bug, three hands shot in the air.

"Oh, alright," said Grandpa, "we'll go a little further and see where this secret trail leads to."

Sheriff Perkins and Doc Barns had been on the trail for two days looking for Jed and Clem. The trail had grown cold and no tracks could be found on the rocky ground. Sheriff Perkins was about to give up and head home when he noticed something shiny off in the distance. A side trail led to a level spot where the sun was glistening on an object high up in a tree. When they reached it, they were stunned at what they saw. A campsite that looked like a tornado had ran through it. Everywhere, torn pieces of sleeping bags and canvas hung in the trees. What had caught their eye was a shiny buckle from a canteen strap.

"What do you think did this?" asked Doc Barns. "And who's camp do you think it was? Jed and Clem's?"

"I don't know," answered the Sheriff. "This is really a mess." He looked down at the campfire and scratched his head. "Whatever happened here is sure strange. Look at the way the fire pit was even torn to pieces. Every creature I know of is afraid of fire."

They began looking for clues to find out who the camp belonged to. After a few minutes, Doc let out a yell. "Over here sheriff, look at this!" He held up a rifle that had the barrel twisted into a "U" shape. Then he read the engraving on the stock. 'Clem Johnson.' They knew they had the answer to one of their questions, It was Jed and Clem's camp alright. After a thorough search, they could find no sign of bodies or of any blood. "This sure is a strange one," said the Doc, shaking his head. "I don't see how anyone could have gotten away from whatever did this but there's no sign of them anywhere. Another strange thing about this is the claw marks. It looks like a bear made some of the marks but others don't look like any animal I've ever seen. There's only one single claw mark on the trees and they're way higher that a normal bear could reach."

The words had no sooner left Doc's mouth when it dawned on him. Single Claw! Maybe there was something to this tale after all.

It wouldn't be until they got back to Sawdust Springs that they would learn what happened at this torn up campsite.

The Sheriff and Doc decided to head back home after not finding any sign of Jed and Clem. What a surprise when they arrived back at Sawdust Springs and found them waiting at the Sheriff's office. They told a story of a giant bear attacking them for no reason and how they ran in the darkness, fell off a cliff into the river, built a makeshift raft and drifted back to town. Though they didn't find Rawhide Jake and collect the reward, they considered themselves mighty lucky just to be alive.

———⟫⟨⟩⟪———

Grandpa was in the lead as he and his grandchildren began exploring the hidden trail. At first it was flat and easy going, a little bushy but not difficult at all. Grandpa wondered who had made the trail and why they had tried to conceal it. For years, back in his younger days, he had traveled the main trail heading into Bear Mountain hauling firewood and thought he knew every inch of it.

"I've never seen this before, I think we're the first ones to discover this hidden trail," said Grandpa.

"Yeah, I sure wonder who built it," added Aria.

Up ahead they could hear the sound of rushing water.
"Is that the Caribou River I hear?" asked Aria.

"Must be," answered Grandpa."Probably where this
trail dead-ends. There normally are steep rock cliffs on
each side of that river and no way to cross it this far up."

Sure enough, in about ten minutes they had reached
the river and were looking down the deep gorge.

"Looks like this is as far as we go," said Grandpa."

"That's strange," said Taven. "Why would anyone go
to all the trouble to built a trail that leads to a dead end?"
Grandpa was about to answer when he noticed another
brush pipe similar to the one at the beginning of the trail.
As he began to clear it away,he was amazed at what he
found. Instead of ending at the river, a narrow ledge had
been chiseled out of solid rock along the cliff wall several
hundred feet above the turbulent river.

"Jumping horny toads! look at that!" exclaimed
Maddox. "Let's see where it goes."

"Not so fast there little partner, we're not mountain
goats you know. My job is to make sure you survive the
summer in one piece." Grandpa was not going to do anything dangerous that would risk their lives.

Then Aria noticed some steel hooks fastened to the
rock wall about every ten feet. "Look Grandpa,those
must be for tying safety rope. If we run my rope through
these, and tie ourselves off, there's no way we could fall."

"You've got a good point Aria, "I'll tell you what, I'll go
along the ledge first and see how safe it is before I decide
about all of us going." He wrapped a rope around his
waist and then tied the other end to one of the hooks that
was fastened to the rock wall. Grandpa slowly stepped

out onto the narrow ledge and soon disappeared as he made his way around the bend. A few minutes later, he started coming back. "What's the matter Grandpa, how come you're coming back so soon?" asked Taven.

"You're never going to believe what I found at the end of the trail."

" Tell us Grandpa, what was it?" The kids could hardly contain their curiosity.

"Well," said Grandpa, just around the bend, someone's built a suspension bridge across the river. And to my surprise, it looks in excellent condition." He knew it would be heartbreaking to turn back now after coming this far. After giving strict instruction, he tied everyone off and they began cautiously walking along the narrow ledge, hugging the cliff wall closer than a mother hugs a baby. Grandpa knew there was no way they could fall, being tied off, or he would never have kept going.

"Wow, this really is an adventure," said Maddox. "Wait till my friends back home hear what we've done!"

Little did they know, but the real adventure was just beginning. Even though walking on a narrow ledge high above a raging river was probably the scariest thing they had ever done, much more danger awaited them. Just looking down into the deep gorge took their breath away. Were they ever glad to reach the suspension bridge. A new kind of fear gripped them when they stepped onto the bridge and it began to sway back and forth.

"It's OK," said Grandpa. "Suspension bridges are made to sway like this". Taven couldn't help having a little fun by bouncing on the bridge. "Stop it, Taven!" yelled Aria. "You're making us all nervous." Slowly, they inched their way across the creaking, swaying bridge. What a relief it was when they reached the other side and stood on solid ground again.

After a much-needed break with some more Trail Mix, they were ready to continue their exploration. They hadn't gone very far when all of a sudden, they heard a roar from some kind of strange animal off in the distance. They all froze with fright.

"What was that ?" asked Maddox.

"I don't know," answered Grandpa. "Never heard a sound like that before. Whatever it was, it sounded big".

"I'm glad it was far away," said Aria.

"Me too" said grandpa, "Let's keep moving and find a good place to make camp before it gets dark."

"Yeah," said Taven, "Let's start the campfire as soon as we get there. That'll keep any wild animals away."

CHAPTER 3

DANGEROUS SHELTER

They had followed the trail for about twenty minutes when they rounded a bend and to their surprise, it dead-ended at a box canyon with steep, rock walls towering high above them on all sides.

"Looks like this is the end of the trail," said Grandpa. "I wonder why anyone would go to all the trouble of building a trail to this desolate place? It just doesn't make sense." Grandpa scratched his head wondering who had built the trail and why. "I don't see any indication that mining or logging ever took place here," as he scanned the steep rock walls. "What could be so special about this box canyon?"

"I don't know Grandpa, but can we go exploring before it gets dark and look for clues?" asked Aria.

"I suppose, but don't be gone long, I want some help setting up camp."

Off they went, scrambling over rocks and brush, looking for clues that might solve the mystery of this strange place.

About ten minutes later,they heard it again, the strange roar from some kind of wild animal, only this time it sounded much closer. Grandpa hollered to the children to come back to camp. He was worried that something might be following them. The only firearm he had was a Colt 22, six- shot revolver, a good gun for small game but not much use for large animals. The kids didn't need to be called twice. The sound of the strange creature sent chills down their back. Aria and Maddox ran back at the same time.

"Where's Taven?" asked Grandpa.

"I'm not sure," answered Aria, "The last time I saw him he was over by those rock piles."

Grandpa called as loud as he could, "Taven! Taven! where are you?" Turning to the other children, he instructed them to stay at the campsite while he went looking for him. "Don't you worry," encouraged Grandpa, "I'll be right back."

The children huddled together, fearful of the strange noise that was coming there way. Grandpa searched in the direction where Taven was last seen, but found nothing. He was just about to look elsewhere, when suddenly Taven appeared, just like a magic act.

"Grandpa, are you looking for me? I heard you call a minute ago."

"A minute ago! I've been hollering at the top of my lungs for the last ten minutes. Where have you been?"

"I'm sorry, Grandpa, but I couldn't hear you. Look at what I discovered." Taven stepped behind a boulder and disappeared again. Grandpa curiously looked around the rock and saw nothing but a small cave with an opening just big enough for a person to squeeze through. Taven popped out of the cave. "See Grandpa, Isn't this neat?"

The roar was heard again and this time there was no doubt. Whatever was making that terrible sound, was getting closer and would soon be upon them.

"You stay here Taven, I'll go back to the campsite and get the other kids." When he reached them, he gave orders to grab their backpacks and stay close to him. There was no time to explain. They ran back to the cave as fast as they could. "Quick, everyone, get inside this cave. We haven't a moment to lose." They scrambled into the cave just as the giant creature arrived at the box canyon. Its roar was deafening. The ground shook as he walked over to their campsite, searching for them.

"Jumping horny toads," whispered Maddox. "That was close. What in the world is that anyway?"

"I don't know," answered Grandpa, "Sounds like a very, very large bear. I'm just glad Taven found this cave or we'd be toast right now."

Grandpa knew the best thing to do was to stay in the cave until that creature went away.

"How far do you think this cave goes?" asked Aria."

"I don't know," answered Grandpa, "I'm just glad it's opening is only big enough for us to get through."

Grandpa took candles from his backpack and passed them to everyone. After lighting them Taven looked up with a "Wow! Look at the size of this cave!" The ceiling was so high the light disappeared into the darkness.

"So this must be it," said Grandpa.

"What?" asked Maddox. "What do you mean?"

"Well, this must be the reason for the trail that led to this box canyon. If I'm right,this might be the cave system that runs clear through the mountain. It's been rumored for years about this but nobody believed it. Kids, we might have just discovered 'the lost caves of Bear Mountain.' "

"You mean there really is a passageway through the mountain like the old prospectors have said?" asked Aria.

"Let's find out," said Grandpa. "At least we're safe in here from that creature that was following us."

As they traveled further back into the cave, they would often see a side trail leading off in another direction. At each one of these intersections, Grandpa would mark the trail with a small pile of rocks. This way they could find their way back through the maze of tunnels without getting lost.

"Grandpa," said Taven, "It looks like someone else has been in these caves not long ago. Look at the these footprints." Sure enough, there were fairly fresh footprints on the soft dirt floor. As they were examining the footprints, Maddox spotted a bright object, partially buried. When he picked it up, he hollered with excitement. "Wow, look at this, a gold coin!" The cave echoed his voice back three times. Grandpa studied the coin and a puzzled look came over him.

"What is it Grandpa, where do you think it came from?"

"I don't know," he answered, "but the inscription 'KGC' sure seems familiar. I know I've heard of it somewhere before. I think it has something to do with Confederate soldiers that fought in the Civil War, but why it's in here is surely a mystery."

Searching the surrounding area brought no further findings of gold coins.

"We'd better keep moving," said Grandpa, "I'd like to get out of here before it gets dark outside." He was just about to turn around when Aria saw a strange light way off in the distance.

"What's that?" asked Aria. "Looks like a small candle! Let's check it out. Maybe it belongs to whoever has been using this cave."

As the curious kids got closer, the light got bigger. Now it no longer looked like a candle, but a big lantern.

"I've got a hunch," whispered grandpa, "If I'm right, that light will continue to get bigger the closer we get to it." And sure, enough it did. "Look kids, it's not man-made light at all; it's daylight. We've gone clear through the mountain and come out on the other side. If I'm right, we've reached the back side of Bear Mountain through this cave system!"

They were all glad to breathe fresh air again as they stepped out of the damp, dark cave. In front of them, they saw tall, black poles standing among the lush, green forest.

"What are those, Grandpa?" asked Taven. "They look like big black toothpicks growing among the trees."

"Those are burnt trees, the remains of a forest fire," answered Grandpa. "It looks like a long time ago a large fire burned through this area."

"Hey," said Aria," maybe this is the fire that's talked about in the legend of Single Claw."

"You might be right," agreed Grandpa. "We've come out in a little valley that I'll bet very few people have ever seen."

"Well, someone's seen it," said Maddox. "Look over there next to the side of the mountain."

Off in the distance where the mountain curves around the valley stood a small log cabin and a little barn, surrounded by corrals.

"I can't believe someone's living way out here," said Maddox. "I wonder who it is?"

Just then, the loud crack of thunder shook the skies. Dark rain clouds were forming in the distance and a full-fledged thunderstorm was about to hit. Grandpa recommended they make a run for the cabin before the rains broke loose. That would be a lot better than spending the night in a damp cave.

They ran down the well-used trail from the cave to the cabin and got there just when the rains started to gully wash. Knocking impatiently on the door, they waited for someone to answer. No one came.

"I don't think anyone's home", said Grandpa. "There's not a lantern lit in the whole house." With the rains coming in a torrent, Grandpa tried the door handle. It wasn't locked. He pushed the door slowly open with a creak that added even more suspense to the moment.

"Hello, anybody home?" hollered Grandpa. No answer. Stepping inside, they saw a scene of total destruction. The whole inside of the cabin had been torn to pieces. Tables thrown across the room, legs broken off the chairs and broken dishes scattered everywhere. The cabin was filled with broken wood and debris.

"Wow! What a mess! What do you think happened here?" asked Aria.

Taven was wide eyed, "It looks like a bomb went off. I wonder who's cabin this is?"

"I don't know," answered grandpa, "but we might as well straighten it up a little and get a fire started in the stove. At least we can stay warm and dry." Aria, Taven and Maddox began moving broken furniture and sweeping while Grandpa put the stove pipe back together and started a fire. Before starting to cook dinner he noticed some unusual marks on the logs inside the cabin. Claw marks, but not normal claw marks. There was only a single claw instead of the normal five. Single Claw marks, Single Claw......! Grandpa froze in his thoughts. It was beginning to make sense now. The missing fishermen, Rawhide Jake disappearing, the strange animal sounds at the box canyon, the proof there was an actual forest fire on Bear Mountain, and now the single claw marks on this stranger's cabin.

"What's the matter, Grandpa?" asked Aria. "You've got a serious look on your face."

"Uh, yeah, It's nothing, I was just thinking." With a worried look he helped them move a heavy beam aside and then place it against the door.

"Why'd you do that?" asked Maddox.

"Oh, just a precaution. Don't know how sturdy this lock is after the beating it took." Grandpa kept his real motives quiet so as not to upset the children.

Our little band of explorers had a wonderful meal of beans and cornbread and were ready for sleep after their exciting day. They were glad to have a roof over their heads with such a terrible storm blowing outside.

They placed their sleeping bags on the floor in front of the warm stove and snuggled in for some much needed rest.

Outside in the raging storm, Single Claw, the largest bear in the world, was making his way along a rocky ridge when suddenly he stopped. He raised his head in the wind and sniffed the air. The smell of wood smoke from the little log cabin was drifting in the air. Rage filled his heart as he turned and followed the smoke, determined to find its source.

CHAPTER 4

TRAPPED

The worst thunderstorm in years was unleashing its fury on the back side of Bear Mountain. The heavy rains came down sideways as the fierce winds blew against the little cabin. Thunder and lightning sounded like bombs exploding on a battlefield.

Everyone was grateful for the shelter of the old, abandoned log cabin they had discovered just before the storm broke loose. Their journey through the lost caves of Bear Mountain had left them with extreme fatigue. Sleeping soundly by the cozy, warm, wood stove, they were oblivious to the storm raging outside. It was a miracle that Maddox awoke to the sound of something quietly scratching on the front door.

"Grandpa, Grandpa, wake up. I hear something," whispered a frightened little boy. He continued to shake Grandpa until he slowly opened his eyes. "I hear something scratching at the door."

Groggily, Grandpa slowly rolled over.

"Yeah, what is it Maddox, what's the matter?"

"I hear a scratching sound at the front door. I'm scared."

Grandpa listened but couldn't hear anything that sounded strange.

"It's alright, probably just the wind blowing branches against the cabin door. Go back to sleep now; everything's fine."

Maddox was sure he'd heard something, but maybe Grandpa was right; maybe it was just the wind. Climbing back into his sleeping bag, he couldn't remember ever hearing a storm so fierce. The wind made the cabin creek and groan.

About ten minutes later, Maddox was just starting to go back to sleep when he heard it again, a clawing sound on the front door. Jumping out of his sleeping bag, he ran over to Grandpa's side.

"Grandpa, wake up, I hear that scratching sound again!"

Grandpa rolled over, trying to control his frustration. "Now I told you, it's just the wind. Would you please go back to sleep." Grandpa jerked the sleeping bag over his shoulders and rolled over. He couldn't remember the last time he had been this tired. But just as he began to drift off to sleep, he heard something that sent chills down his spine. Was he dreaming? It didn't sound like the brushing of branches from the wind, but a deliberate, methodical clawing on the cabin door. Then he remembered there weren't any trees around the cabin. It couldn't be branches. He bolted wide awake, listening to something trying to get in through the locked door. His mind raced, what was it? What would be out on a night like this? Was it the same creature that made the strange roaring sounds the day before back at the box canyon? If it was, they were in big trouble. Without losing any more time trying to figure it out, Grandpa rolled out of his sleeping bag and began waking the children. "Quick, get up," he whispered as he gently shook the sleepy children. Maddox didn't need any coaxing since he hadn't gone back to sleep. He was relieved that finally someone else heard the strange noise.

" Taven, grab our sleeping bags and packs and get over to that cellar door." While cleaning up, they had discovered a trap door to the stairs that led under the house. "Lift it up and throw our packs and sleeping bags down into the cellar." "Hurry, we've no time to lose.". Grandpa led the confused kids to the door and helped them down the steep stairs.

"What's happening?,"asked Aria. "What's wrong?"

"No time to explain," said Grandpa. "Just get down in the cellar as quick as you can."

After everyone made it down the steps, Grandpa lowered the trap door behind him. They all huddled together in the cold, dark cellar, not making a sound.

"Something is trying to open the front door," whispered Grandpa. " We should be safe down here, just don't make a sound. We must be quiet as a mouse."

All of a sudden, the house above them exploded with a loud crashing sound. They heard the front door break to pieces as the raging beast forced his way into the cabin. Growling with the same horrible roar they had heard the day before in the box canyon. The creature began looking for the occupants of the cabin. The smell of wood smoke created a murderous rage in him. The noise was terrifying as the large bear tore the cabin apart, looking for Grandpa and his Grandchildren. He knew that humans were in there somewhere, but where? The more he looked the madder he got. Ceiling rafters caved in, walls were shoved out, the damage was tremendous. Listening to this devastation from the cellar sent shivers of fear through everyone. They sat in silence, praying that the trap door wouldn't be discovered. For what seemed like an eternity of twenty minutes, the devastation went on. Then all became silent.

"Has it left?" whispered Taven.

"No," said Grandpa, "I think it's listening for us. Shhhh".

Aria got a panicked look on her face as she felt a sneeze coming on. Ah,Ah, —Grandpa quickly put his hand over her mouth. A few tense moments went by before Aria communicated with her eyes and shook her head, "It's OK now, the sneeze has gone away."

"That was a close one," thought Grandpa.

Another five minutes went by before they heard the killer bear walking across the floor above them and out onto the front porch.

"Is it gone now Grandpa?" whispered Taven.

"Sounds like it, but we'd better stay down here a little longer just to be sure."

————)⟨⟩(————

A grizzled old prospector was leading his donkey and hound dog through the maze of tunnels that wound through Bear Mountain. "Hee Haw, Hee Haw, Hee Haw."

"Now Conniption, you just settle down. We'll take a break in a few minutes if that's what you want."

Rawhide Jake communicated better with his two furry companions than most do with real people. They seemed to understand every word he said. Hambone, a cross between a bloodhound and a black and tan, was the best dog a man could ever want. And Conniption was the best donkey in the world in Rawhide's mind. Hambone's tail wagged happily when he heard the words, "Let's take a break, you can have a treat."

They had been hiding out in the caves for several weeks, ever since Single Claw paid them a visit one night and tried to have them for supper. "The only thing I can figure out," explained Rawhide to Hambone, "is that the stove pipe I wired together came apart in the wind." The cagey old prospector had piped the wood smoke back into a crack in the side of the mountain that led into the cave system. That's how he'd kept it undetected from that bear all these years.

Rawhide Jake had escaped exactly the same way Grandpa and his grandkids did when that bear attacked. He and Hambone had hidden in the cellar till the coast was clear. Conniption ran into the forest and reunited with them a couple days later.

Rawhide was sitting on a rock, finishing off a piece of beef jerky, when all of a sudden he jumped to his feet. "Confound it, look at this! Footprints." How in tarnation did these footprints get here? No one knows this cave system but us." Hambone cocked his head, trying to understand.

"Looks like a grownup and several children."

In all the years of living on the backside of Bear Mountain, he'd never had any intruders. His mind was racing. Somehow, someone must have discovered the hidden entrance at the box canyon. That's the only way they could have gotten into the south end of the caves.

"Come on, Hambone, make yourself useful. Get a scent on this trail and follow it." The eager hound put his nose to the ground and began sniffing the tracks. The implications of the caves being discovered were many. If word got out, the secret about his gold mine would be in jeopardy. Rawhide had kept the lost caves a secret for many years but now it looks like someone else has discovered them. They followed the footprints to where the trail left the caves on the other side of the mountain, close to the log cabin. "Better stop here for the night," murmured Rawhide. "I don't want to leave the safety of these here caves while it's dark outside. Least not until we know if that ornery bar is gone.

————◦)⋘⋙(◦————

Grandpa woke in the cold, dark cellar from a restless night's sleep.

"Wake up everybody. It should be safe to leave now. I haven't heard any sound from that creature for quite a while. I'll go up first and check it out; you guys stay here until I give the all clear."

"Oh Grandpa, please be careful! It might be waiting for us out in the woods," cautioned Maddox.

"What do you think it was anyway?" asked Taven.

"I don't know," said Grandpa, "but if I was a betting man, I'd say we just had a run in with Single Claw."

"Single Claw!" gasped Aria. "Do you really think it was him?" Grandpa explained all the clues that were adding up.

"When I saw the single claw marks on the cabin walls, that cinched it. I can't be 100% sure, but this creature sure matches everything we've heard about him. Finding the remnants of a forest where he might have been burned was another clue. Then there's all the people that keep disappearing on the back side of Bear Mountain. We must be extra careful when we go upstairs."

He started up the stairs and tried to lift the trap door. He strained but the door wouldn't budge. He tried again, putting his back against the door and shoving with all his might. Still the door wouldn't budge.

"What's the matter?" asked Taven. "Why won't the door open?"

"Must be wedged shut," answered Grandpa. "You kids come up here and give me a hand".

They shoved and pushed with all their combined strength but still the door wouldn't move.

"It's got to be a beam, or something very heavy fallen down against the door," said Grandpa.

"What will we do now?" asked Aria. "Are we trapped?"

"I'm afraid we are," said Grandpa with a discouraged look. "Let's go back down the stairs and think this over."

Their place of refuge had turned into a prison and Grandpa knew he had to find a way out. He sat down, leaning against the cellar wall. Trying not to look worried, he needed to reassure the children as they gathered around him.

"Now don't worry. We're going to find a way out of here. Check your packs and see how much food and water we have."

After searching their backpacks, they came up with three full canteens of water, a bag of trail mix, six candy bars, a bag of potato chips and a small bag of flour.

"If we ration this, we'll be OK for several days," consoled Grandpa. "That should give us enough time to find a way out of here."

"I can't believe this is happening," said Taven, "We're trapped like animals in a cage!"

"What if we can't get out?" said Maddox. "We'll die down here and nobody knows where we are. We don't even know where we are."

"Whose cabin is this anyway?" asked Aria.

"I don't know," said Grandpa, "but I do know this; we're not going to die. Somehow, we'll get out of here, I promise you. The most important thing we can do now is pray. God will help us."

He was reassuring himself as much as the kids as things didn't look good. His job right now was to keep everyone calm and not to panic. He knew that panic is the number one reason people don't survive in dangerous situations. Lighting a candle brought a glow of warmth and security. He found a piece of broken wood and began to scrape at the cellar wall.

"What are you doing," asked Aria.

"Just seeing how hard this dirt is. We might be able to tunnel our way out. Grab a board and help me dig."

All the kids joined in and dug with determination. Progress was slow as the ground was filled with rock, but at least it gave them something to keep their minds off their hopeless situation.

Maddox went to the back of the basement looking for a stick to dig with when suddenly, he let out a squeal of surprise. They all turned to see what the commotion was about. Thinking it might be a snake, grandpa ran over to the frightened child.

"Now back away real slow. No quick moves."

"Why?" asked Maddox, spinning around with a smile on his face.

He held up an old leather pouch. "Look at what I found!"

Grandpa took the pouch and noticed that it was extremely heavy for its size. After peering in, he reached into the pouch and pulled out a handful of gold coins. Relief came over everyone.

"Look at all this gold, we're rich!" exclaimed Maddox, "And look at this, they all have the same inscription as the coin we found back in the caves…, 'KGC'. Can we keep them?" Maddox asked, "Can we?"

"First, we'll have to find out whose they are before we can claim them., Otherwise it would be stealing."

"Oh Grandpa, that's not fair."

"What's right is always more important than what's fair," explained Grandpa. "This does explain one thing though. Whoever lost that gold coin in the cave must be the same person that owns this cabin."

The question is, ``Who is he and is he still alive?"

Aria got them all back to reality by reminding them of their predicament. "A lot of good being rich will do us," she cried with tears flowing down her face. "All the money in the world won't get us out of here. Right now, food and water are more valuable than gold."

"That's right," said Grandpa. "Before we get to worrying over who's gold this is, we'd better keep digging." He couldn't help but think of all the lives that have been ruined over the love of money.

All day long they dug in the hard soil but by evening they had only gone about a foot. The situation didn't look good, and despair was setting in.

"Grandpa, it'll take a week to dig our way out at the pace we're going." complained Taven. "And by that time, we'll be out of supplies."

Grandpa just said, "We need to keep on digging and praying."

CHAPTER 5

SURPRISE VISITORS

Grandpa stopped digging in the escape tunnel when he noticed that the kids were listening to something. Their ears were a lot keener than his.

"What is it? What do you hear?" asked Grandpa.

"I don't know," said Taven., "Maybe it's Single Claw."

"Something is out there alright," said Maddox. "I can hear something coming towards the cabin."

Grandpa blew out the candle and gathered them in the far corner of the basement. "Be real quiet," he whispered. "That bear might be coming back for us."

As they hunkered together in the dark cellar, they could hear something coming closer and closer. Fear was starting to grip them when all of a sudden they heard a loud and clear, "Hee Haw, Hee Haw, Hee Haw."

With looks that expressed, 'what was that'? They turned to Grandpa.

A smile slowly crept over Grandpa's face as he said, "One thing's for sure, that's not a bear."

"Hee Haw," was heard again.

"Sounds more like a donkey to me," said Grandpa.

Then they could hear someone talking. "Now settle down Conniption, It's alright, that old bar's long gone."

"Someone's up there, we're saved!" shouted Aria.

Our trapped survivors began shouting and yelling at the top of their lungs. Then a hound dog began howling back at all the commotion.

"Help, help, get us out of here!" shouted the children. Rawhide Jake was as surprised as they were.

"Who in tar nation are you? And how'd you get trapped in my cellar?" hollered the old prospector.

Grandpa thought he recognized the voice. "Is that you Rawhide?"

"It shore is, but who are you?" he hollered.

"It's me, Buck, your old friend from Sawdust Springs, and I've got my three grandkids with me."

"Well if that doesn't beat an egg sucken dog," yelled Rawhide. "My old friend Buck! How'd you get trapped in my basement?"

"Help get us out of here and I'll explain everything," answered grandpa.

Rawhide was dismayed at all the destruction he saw inside his cabin. Working his way through the broken boards he took one and pried a heavy beam off the cellar door. When he lifted the door open our trapped survivors scrambled out faster than scarred jack rabbits. The children began hugging and thanking Rawhide, then they hugged his companions, Hambone, the best hound dog in the world and Conniption, the cutest and friendliest donkey you'll ever see. Those two critters were surprised from all the attention they were getting but they loved every minute of it. Hambone began howling and jumping in the air with excitement. His tongue was licking them so fast, the children had to cover their faces. Then he went over and licked Conniption on the nose, as if to say to the little donkey, "you're still my best friend." The daylight, fresh air and freedom brought everyone back to high spirits.

"Man, are we glad you came along," said Grandpa. "We thought we were goners. How in the world did you find us in this out-of-the-way place, anyway?"

"Out-of-the-way place!" snapped Rawhide. "Why, this is my cabin! The question should be, what brought you way up here and how in the world did you find my homestead?"

They sat down on the porch steps and Grandpa explained everything.

"It started when you didn't come in for supplies this spring and Sheriff Perkins started looking for you. He even set up a reward for anyone who could find you."

Rawhide got a surprised look on his face. "I didn't think anybody was that concerned over a worn out old prospector."

"Well, they are and that's why we started looking for you. We started out on the trail to Bear Mountain and accidentally discovered the hidden trail leading to the box canyon. It was a miracle we found the entrance to the caves and escaped a large bear just as he was closing in on us. When we got through the mountain we saw your cabin and took shelter from that thunder storm that passed here a couple days ago. That night a bear attacked us. We think it's the same one that was following us and is the one they call Single Claw."

Rawhide confirmed their suspicion. Standing bow legged with his hands on his hips, the short, sturdy prospector let out a sigh.

"Horse feathers! Buck, It is Single Claw, and you and your grandkids are lucky to be alive."

Maddox couldn't help but ask, "If that was Single Claw, then how have you managed to survive up here all these years?"

"That's a good question, little feller," smiled Rawhide. "You just have to be smarter than that big overgrown fur ball." Rawhide reminded them again that it's the smell of smoke that attracts that bear, and as long as you didn't start a fire, you'd be OK. He showed them how for years he had run his stove pipe into the side of the mountain through a crack to hide the wood smoke. "When a storm knocked it down one night, that's when things went cadi-whompas."

"Then the money must belong to you?" asked Maddox.

"What money?" questioned Rawhide.

"The gold coins I found in the cellar and the one I found in the cave,"

Rawhide got a worried look on his face. "I should have been more careful. Never thought anyone would find me up here after all these years. I am relieved though that the footprints I found in the caves were yours and that you're the ones that found my cabin. Your Grandpa is the most honest man I know."

"By the way," asked Grandpa, "what do the letters ' KGC' mean on those coins?"

Rawhide paused, looking very serious. Realizing they had discovered his long held secret he decided he might as well explain everything. "Before I tell you, I want the whole kit and cabuttle of you to promise you'll never tell another soul as long as you live. Is that a deal?"

"Sure," said Grandpa, "we'll give you our word, won't we kids?"

"You bet, Grandpa," They all nodded their heads and pledged to never let another soul know the secret of the gold coins.

"Well then," continued Rawhide, "Have you ever heard of the Knights of the Golden Circle?

Grandpa thought for a moment, rubbing his chin. "Why, yes," he said, "It's coming back to me. That's what those initials KGC stand for, don't they. Knights of the Golden Circle."

"You darn tooten," said Rawhide.

"What are, or should I say, who are the Knights of the Golden Circle?" asked Aria.

"Well," began Rawhide, "I'll start by saying, no one believes they ever really existed. They think they're being bam-boozled by some shikester. I didn't believe either until I discovered a large stash of gold coins hidden back in one of those caves. The legend of the KGC goes like this. At the end of the Civil War, the south knew they were going to lose the war. The president of the southern states, Jefferson Davis, devised a plan to save all their gold from falling into the hands of the Union Army. This gave them hope and resources so they could rebuild the South sometime in the future and rise to power again. So they melted down all their gold into coins and engraved them with the initials KGC. They divided the gold up into twelve separate boxes and entrusted them to twelve loyal men. Each man would guard his box with his life. This way if one got discovered, they wouldn't lose them all. These men were called the Knights of the Golden Circle. They were told to take the gold to the far north where it would never be discovered. Once they found a secure hiding place, they were told to make a coded map and send it back to President Davis. When the timing was right, they would be called back to the south with their precious cargo. The problem was, they were never called back."

"What happened to the Knights?" asked Aria.

"Well, as the years went by and they grew old, they entrusted their secret mission to their children before they died. They in turn would entrust it to their children. From generation to generation, they kept hoping that the South would someday call for the gold. Evidently, the knight that guarded the stash I found, died unexpectedly, before he could entrust it to others. He died in the caves, probably of smallpox.

His skeleton is still laying in the caves."

"I'm beginning to get the picture," said Grandpa. "In order to keep the secret of the Knights of the Golden Circle from being discovered, you would melt down a few gold coins and turn them into nuggets whenever you needed supplies. That way, people would think you have a gold mine up here instead of lost Confederate gold."

"That's right," nodded Rawhide. "Once I realized the Knights of the Golden Circle were real, I couldn't trust anyone. Other Knights could be close by that we don't even know about."

"How much do you figure you have?" asked Tavern.

"Probably several million dollars," answered Rawhide. "More than I'll ever spend in my lifetime. I've been thinking lately, I'm not getting any younger; what will I do with all that money? I certainly don't need that much. As long as I have my cabin, my donkey and my hound dog, I'm happy. I'd be willing to share it with you as long as you agree to my terms. I can't think of more trustworthy, honorable people than Buck and his family."

"Jumping Horney toads," cried Maddox, "we are rich!"

"Now hold on there," interrupted Grandpa., "Rawhide didn't say how much he would give us. Let's listen to what his terms are."

"Well," began Rawhide, "I was thinking of using the gold to help people in need. You know, like widows, orphans, the injured and sick. You folks have more opportunity to see who's in need than I do. Living on the back side of Bear Mountain doesn't lend itself to a lot of company. Whenever you come across someone that's in genuine need, we'll all get together and decide on the amount to give. That will make us all accountable to one other."

"That's a wonderful plan and mighty generous of you, Rawhide," commended Grandpa. "We promise we'll do all we can to honor your wishes. There is one thing though. The only other person that should be in on this is the kid's Grandma. Is that O.K. With you?"

"Of course it is. I should have thought of it myself. If you can't trust your family, who can you trust?" Rawhide instructed them to use the money wisely and that it was also there to help with personal supplies or anything else they might need to fulfill this special mission.

"Grandpa," said Taven, "this really is turning out to be one of the greatest adventures we've ever had." All the children were so excited they gave Grandpa, Rawhide, Hambone, and Conniption another big round of hugs.

The excitement of their newfound riches was suddenly interrupted with a frightening sound off in the distance. The loud roar of a gigantic bear!

"It's Single Claw," yelled Rawhide. "Grab your gear and high tail it to the caves as quickly as you can! In a flash, he ran behind the cabin, grabbed Conniption by the harness, whistled for Hambone and signaled for everyone to follow. They scrambled like jack rabbits up the trail leading back into the caves.

The thunderous roar was getting closer!

"Hurry," hollered Grandpa, "he's gaining on us!"

Hambone let out a howl. "Quiet, Hambone, you're going to give away our location," snapped Rawhide.

It was only a quarter mile to the narrow cave entrance, but it seemed much further when being pursued by a killer bear. The roar came again.

"He's closing the gap!" hollered Rawhide, "Keep moving"

They were already running as fast as they could, but Single Claw was gaining ground. Up ahead they could see the narrow opening of the cave. It was just wide enough for the little donkey to squeeze through. The safety of the caves was only a hundred feet away.

"Run, faster!" yelled Grandpa as he reached down and grabbed Maddox's hand, "We're going to make it!" He had no sooner spoken when Single Claw appeared behind them. "Quick, we've no time to lose!"

Out of breath, Aria was first to reach the cave entrance. She leaned over and dove through the narrow opening with Maddox and Grandpa right behind her. Next came Rawhide with Conniption and Hambone. Taven, who had been helping Rawhide with his donkey, was the last one in line. When Rawhide made it through the cave entrance, he turned around to help Taven... but he wasn't there. Just fifty feet from the cave's entrance, Taven had tripped and hit his head on a rock. Being stunned from the fall, he was slow to get up, Single Claw was quickly closing the gap.

"Get up! Get up!," they all screamed. It was like a nightmare unfolding before their eyes in slow motion. They could see Taven wasn't going to make it to the safety of the cave. In a split second, Single Claw stood towering over his helpless prey. Taven froze with fear as he looked up and saw the huge bear standing over him. Single Claw roared a deafening roar, stood up on his hind legs and raised his paw for the death blow. Then something happened that we'll remember for the rest of our lives. Hambone let out a growl and sprang from the cave like he was shot out of a cannon. He distracted the bear by running around and around him in tight circles, barking, growling and nipping every chance he got. Single Claw didn't know what to think. Then, like a steel-jawed trap, Hambone clamped his teeth right onto that bear's bottom. Rooooooar! Single Claw spun around trying to reach the dog, but Hambone hung on for the ride of his life, swinging through the air like a carnival ride. Grandpa saw his chance. He darted out of the cave and snatched up Taven while Hambone had Single Claw distracted.

With the speed of a racehorse, they ran back to the safety of the cave while the bear was trying to get that dog off his bottom. Single Claw spun in circles trying to reach Hambone. Finally, the tired dog couldn't hold on any longer. Letting go, he sailed through the air and landed hard on some rocks. With a yelp, he laid still. Single Claw slowly walked over to the helpless dog and was about to finish him off when, BOOM! The crack of gunfire echoed off the mountains. Rawhide Jake had pulled his rifle from Conniption's saddle bag and unloaded it on that monster bear. The hide on Single Claw was so thick there was little chance of hurting him, but the shear surprise and noise was enough to send him running back into the woods. He'd had enough of this wild and crazy bunch. Rawhide ran over to Hambone and carefully scooped him up in his arms. " No mangy bar's gonna hurt my Hambone," said Rawhide, as he proudly carried him back to the cave and laid him down. "You're the bravest dog I've ever seen."

CHAPTER 6

THE LOST CAVES

B ack at Sawdust Springs, Grandma was worried about her overdue campers. They were only supposed to be gone for two or three days. This was day number four and it wasn't like Grandpa to keep them out that long, unless something bad happened, she thought. She pulled on her boots and put on her bonnet before heading out the door to Sheriff Perkins office. He needed to know about the camping trip to Bear Mountain that Grandpa and the Grand kids were on."I know I'm sounding silly," explained Grandma, " but it isn't like Buck to be gone longer than he says he'll be. I'm terribly worried that something bad has happened.

Sheriff Perkins got a worried look on his face. "When did you say they left?" he asked.

"Last Wednesday, early in the morning," answered Grandma.

"If that doesn't beat all ! I must have just missed them! It was around ten o'clock, Wednesday when I posted the warning sign," said the sheriff.

"Warning sign! What warning sign?" asked Grandma.

The sheriff explained everything to her, how Clem and Jed had been attacked by a huge bear, that Rawhide Jake was still missing, and about the two fishermen that had disappeared earlier in the spring. Sheriff Perkins paced the floor with a worried look." There are just too many strange things happening that point to Single Claw."

"Single Claw!" exclaimed Grandma. "Are you telling me he's real?"

"Now don't worry," consoled the sheriff as he helped Grandma sit down in a chair. "We don't know if it's really him or not. I just want to be cautious, that's all. That's why I posted a warning sign to keep people away from Bear Mountain. I sure wish I'd known Buck was planning a camping trip up there with your grandkids. Let's give it one more day and hope they get back. I'm sorry if I've caused you more worry."

"It's alright," said Grandma, fighting back tears, "it's not your fault."

Grandma went back to her cabin and began praying harder than she'd ever prayed before.

The caves of Bear Mountain provided much needed protection for our weary group of adventurers. All of the entrances to the caves were too small for a bear the size of Single Claw to enter.

Exhausted from their narrow escape, the grand kids rested against the cave wall while Grandpa and Rawhide cooked up a pot of beans and cornbread. The kids stroked and praised Hambone, the bravest dog in all the world in their opinion. After all, he did risk his life to save Taven. The injured dog rested peacefully. Sprawled out on his back enjoying a belly rub and soaking up all the attention.

"Will he be alright?" asked Aria.

"Oh, he'll be alright," answered Rawhide. "Looks like he might just have a bad sprained leg, but no broken bones. After he rests a bit, I'll bandage him up and make a stretcher so we can carry him."

The kids smothered him with more affection by feeding him some of their trail mix. Hambone's eyes and tail said "thank you." It was a good sign.

"Come and get it," ordered Rawhide. He spooned the beans over hot slabs of corn bread fresh from his Dutch oven. It was a meal fit for a king. When they were finished, Rawhide took his plate over to Hambone to lick it clean. Everyone followed his example which was perfectly alright with Hambone.

"This will do till we get some water tomorrow to wash them properly," explained Rawhide as he tucked the dishes back into his saddle bags.

Grandpa explained to Rawhide that they really needed to get back to Sawdust Springs as soon as possible. "We're overdue and I know Grandma will be worried about us."

"No problem," said Rawhide, "We should make it back by tomorrow easily, but while we're here, there's something I want to show you."

Rawhide led them deeper into the caves. They followed the soft glow of his lantern through a labyrinth of dark tunnels. The kids took turns carrying Hambone on his improvised stretcher.

"How do you keep from getting lost in here?" asked Maddox. "Never think much about it," answered Rawhide. "Been in here so much I know every nick and cranny of this place. If I ever did get turned around, old Hambone here could sniff our way out."

They hadn't gone much further, when just around a bend their eyes caught sight of something that made them gasp with fright. They froze in their tracks.

"What is, or should I say, who is that?" asked Grandpa.

Up ahead, laying against a large rock, was a skeleton wearing a torn and tattered Confederate uniform. One hand was holding a sword pointing off into the darkness.

"I'm scared!" said Maddox.

"Me too." said Aria and Taven in unision.

"This is what I wanted to show you," said Rawhide. "There's nothing to be scared about. It is kinda scary looking but this old soldier can't hurt anyone. This is the Confederate soldier I told you about that died in these caves years ago. When I first came across him, I didn't think much about it. Just felt sorry for the old fellow. The only thing I found was a map he was working on, showing how to get to these caves. Probably planned to send it back to the south before he got sick. Then one day, while prospecting in the caves, I happened to notice his sword. How it seemed to be pointing to something. It dawned on me that maybe he was trying to say something before he died. My curiosity got the best of me and I went searching in the direction his sword was pointing. Wound up in a dead end tunnel and was about to turn around when I noticed a gold coin laying in the dirt. The old soldier was trying to tell me something alright. You'll understand better when you see it. Come with me and I'll show you what I found."

Rawhide led them down a dark passageway, their shadows dancing off the walls from his kerosene lantern. When he got to the end of the tunnel he turned and asked, " Well, here it is. Do you see it?"

"See what?" said Grandpa.

"I don't see anything either," said Aria.

"Look hard, that's just what I thought, too, when I first came to this place," said Rawhide.

They all examined the rock and dirt and couldn't see anything unusual. "All I see is a dead-end tunnel," said Taven.

Then Grandpa noticed something. "Hey, this large rock looks out of place, like it's been placed here. It's not like the others laying around it."

"You're right," said Rawhide. "It has been placed here, by that old soldier."

Rawhide put his shoulder to the rock and shoved with all his might, revealing a small opening behind it. "Take a look in here," he said as he held the lantern up close.

When they looked in, they couldn't believe what they saw. Gold, more gold than they had ever imagined! Glistening in the light were thousands of gold coins. They were speechless. All except Maddox who let loose with another, "Jumping horny toads!"

Finally, Grandpa spoke. "Rawhide, you've entrusted us with your life's treasure by showing us this secret. I promise, we won't ever break that trust."

"I know," said Rawhide as he rolled the rock back into place. "Like I said before, I believe you and your family

have integrity and honor. That's why I can trust you."
Rawhide took a rag and dusted their tracks away from
the rock, concealing the treasure. "Just a precaution in
case someone does stumble onto these caves. You can see
now why that old soldier built a secret trail to this place.
If the caves were discovered, the best hiding place in the
world would have been lost."

"You mean he's the one who built the trail and suspension bridge over the river that leads to the box canyon?"
asked Taven.

"You got that right." answered Rawhide. "And he did
a pretty good job Keeping it hidden for years. The only
reason I found it was when Hambone chased a rabbit into
it and I went looking for him."

"Rawhide," said Aria, "don't you think it would be a
good idea if we moved the sword so it doesn't look like
it's pointing somewhere? Just in case someone else ever
discovers him?"

"Good idea" said Rawhide, "Never thought about that.
I suppose if you found the caves, someone else could too."

They went back to the skeleton and gently laid his
sword down by his side. "Now old timer, you won't
be sharing your secret with anyone else," whispered
Rawhide reverently.

They spent that night in the caves and came to the
opening at the box canyon early the next morning. The
only tricky part now was crossing the suspension bridge
and traversing the narrow, rock ledge high above the
Caribou River. "How will Conniption make it through
this narrow trail?" asked Maddox.

"You won't have to worry about him," said Rawhide. "He's more surefooted than any of us. Fortunately, the old Confederate soldier that built this trail made it just wide enough for his donkey to cross."

Sure enough, when they came to the narrow trail, Conniption scampered over it like it was nothing. Grandpa walked backwards holding Hambone's stretcher while Rawhide carried the other end. They were all relieved to make it safely to the other side. From there it was all downhill to Sawdust Springs. "We should be home in about four more hours," said Grandpa.

"Yea!" shouted the grand kids, as they hurried along the trail with renewed energy. It was around three o'clock when they rounded the last bend and could see their little homestead nestled alongside the Caribou River. "That must be what heaven looks like," said Aria. "I can't wait to tell Grandma about our trip!"

They were practically running. Holding on to each other to keep from stumbling, the weary, worn travelers hurried toward home. Grandma heard them hollering and came out to see what all the commotion was about. Off in the distance, she saw three excited children, two adults carrying a dog on a stretcher and one donkey. When she realized it was her overdue family, she let out a loud shout of joy and relief. Her heart was filled with gratitude for answered prayer as tears rolled down her cheeks. She flung off her apron and ran toward them with open arms. When they met, Grandma gave everyone a big bear hug. They were all talking ninety miles an hour telling about their experience.

"Slow down" said Grandma, "I can't understand a word you're saying. I've got an idea. Let's wait till after dinner to explain everything. I'll invite Sheriff Perkins over so he can hear firsthand from everyone just what happened back there on that mountain." Grandma knew that after all the effort the Sheriff had made to find Rawhide, he'd be thrilled to see him safe and sound.

CHAPTER 7

THE MISSION

It was a full house that evening. Grandma had invited Sheriff Perkins to join Rawhide Jake and the rest of her family. She cooked one of the best dinners they had ever tasted. Skillet fried chicken, mashed potatoes and gravy, corn on the cob, homemade sourdough bread, tossed green salad and iced tea–all topped off with her famous apple pie and a scoop of ice cream. Not many people can make a wood cook stove perform like she does. Needless to say, after dinner, everyone found a comfortable chair and relaxed in front of the fireplace. Even Hambone sprawled out on the throw rug, acting like the guest of honor. Enjoying all the attention he was getting from his injured leg.

"Well, Sheriff, I suppose you're anxious to hear our story," said Grandpa.

"I sure am. I was beginning to doubt I'd ever see the likes of you again."

Grandpa asked Rawhide to go first, then he would share his story, being careful not to mention anything about the gold, of course. Sheriff Perkins listened with great interest while jotting down some notes. Rawhide explained how Single Claw tore up his cabin and how he narrowly escaped. Then Grandpa told his story about finding Rawhide's cabin. No mention was made about the secret trail or the caves.

"That's an incredible story," said the Sheriff. "This proves without a doubt that Single Claw is real. You guys are the first ones to encounter that killer bear more than once and live to tell about it. I think the whole town would like to hear what I just heard. Let's plan a town meeting at the community hall this Saturday night. Oh, and before I forget, here's the hundred dollar reward for finding Rawhide." He pulled an envelope from his shirt pocket.

"That's OK," said Grandpa, waving it aside. He's actually the one who found and rescued us. Why don't you give it to someone like the widow Larson. She could use it and needs it a lot more than we do."

"You bet!" said Taven. " Let's give it to her."

Grandma beamed with pride at her family's charitable attitude.

After Sheriff Perkins left, Rawhide thought it was time to tell Grandma about the gold. After all, she is part of the family. At first, she couldn't believe it, she thought they were teasing her with a tall tale, but after everyone had convincingly told their part of the story, all she could do was stand there looking amazed, holding her hand over her mouth.

Rawhide asked if he could stay for a couple of weeks to give Hambone's leg a chance to heal. Of course it was O.K. He always slept in the hay loft anyway and was no trouble at all. This would also give him time to pick up his needed supplies in town. The other thing he asked was to skip the town meeting. "I've never had a hankering for public speaking or large gatherings. That's the way us ornery prospectors are," he said with a smile.

Saturday night came and there was a feeling of celebration in the air. The whole town turned out to welcome our lost friends home. A huge banner was hung on the town hall that said, "Welcome home Rawhide, Buck and the Grandkids". In small print were the names, Aria, Taven and Maddox. To their surprise, a reporter from the *Far North Gazette Newspaper* showed up and took pictures of them for the next edition.

After a wonderful potluck dinner, Mayor Bud Morgan stepped up to the platform. "Friends, the reason we invited you out tonight was not only to show our gratitude for Buck and his grandkids safe return, but also to give them an opportunity to share their amazing story that I guarantee you'll want to hear. Let's give them a good old hometown welcome!"

The applause was heart-warming as the three Grandkids and Grandpa came up to the platform. When it was quiet, Grandpa began to share his story. You could have heard a pin drop as he explained how the Legend of Single Claw is real. Full attention was given to every word about the largest, meanest bear in the world. The seriousness of what they were hearing began to soak in. Their quiet, peaceful community was now faced with the startling reality of a killer bear called Single Claw. When he finished, hands shot up everywhere. Questions shouted out from the crowd.

"What's going to happen now?" asked one of the mothers holding a small child. "Will we ever be safe from that dangerous bear?"

"That's a good question," chimed in Mayor Morgan. "What do you suggest we do to protect ourselves from an animal like that?"

Grandpa explained that it's the smell of wood smoke that usually sets him off. He told how Rawhide Jake had lived for years right in the backyard of that bear's territory and never had a problem until his stove pipe fell down. He had hid the smoke for years by piping it into a nearby cave. As long as you don't start a campfire on the backside of Bear Mountain, you'll be alright, Grandpa assured them.

"And remember, he's never come close to Sawdust Springs, in fact, he's never even been seen as close as Loon Lake, which is several miles from here. His home is on the other side of Bear Mountain." This reassured the townspeople somewhat, but concern was still on their faces.

It was then that Grandpa felt a strong impression. It was an impression that would change his life and the lives of his grandkids forever. Could this idea be from God? He wasn't sure, at least not at first because it seemed so ridiculous. Finally, the pleasant evening ended with heartwarming handshakes. But all the way home, Grandpa couldn't shake the thoughts he was having. Thoughts of him and his grandkids defending the weak and helpless from the killer bear called Single Claw. How could this happen? How could an aging grandfather and three young grandkids stand up against the largest, meanest bear in the world? Then he remembered the story of a young Shepherd boy standing up against a giant that was many times stronger than himself. He fought him with only a sling and a stone, and he won! One of Grandpa's favorite Bible verses was, "With man it is impossible, but with God all things are possible." If they were to do this, it would definitely have to be from God.

Several days went by before Grandpa mentioned any of this to Grandma and the children. Expecting to see some doubt, he was surprised when no one said a word. "Well, what do you think? Do you think I'm crazy?" asked Grandpa.

"Not at all," said Aria, "In fact, we've been talking about the same thing, about finding some way we could help people that were in danger from that bear."

Even Grandma said she'd been having the same thoughts that Grandpa had. "I think you should do something about helping others," said Grandma. "After all, isn't that one of the reasons we're put here on this earth? My only question is, how are you planning to do it?"

Grandpa took a deep breath and then said, "Well, that's confirmation. Here's what I've been thinking.

You kids are too young to have firearms but that doesn't mean you can't defend yourselves. Medieval weaponry ruled the world for thousands of years. Aria, I want you to become the best shot with a bow and arrow ever seen in the far north. You will become a modern day, Robin Hood. Taven, you'll have a shield, sword and helmet just like the Roman soldiers wore. Maddox, a spear and throwing knives will be your specialty. You'll wear a belt that holds several throwing knives and carry a spear."

"What about you, Grandpa," asked Maddox, "What will you do?"

"I'll carry my Winchester 300 magnum. My hope is that we'll never be faced with hand-to-hand combat like you'll be trained for, but if we do, I want you to be able to defend yourself if something happens to me."

"But Grandpa," said Taven, "It will cost a lot of money for all this equipment." The words had no sooner left his mouth than he remembered the gold. "I've got it! well use some of the gold, right?"

"That's right,", said Grandpa., "First we'll have a meeting with Rawhide for approval., Then, if everyone agrees, we'll buy the best equipment money can buy: a titanium bow with graphite arrows, a carbon fiber shield and helmet with a 440 stainless steel sword, balanced throwing knives with industrial diamond edges, and two tungsten bladed spears with Kevlar handles. I'll also carry a medical kit that would make a doctor proud. It could save the life of someone we find injured by that bear. "Yes, money will not be a hindrance, and we'll call ourselves, 'The Bear Hunters.' The one rule we'll always use is to never kill any animal, even a dangerous bear, if we can avoid it. Our goal will be to save lives, not destroy. To avoid conflict and only fight to defend ourselves or others."

The next day, they met with Rawhide about using some of the money to buy weapons for self-defense. Everyone was in agreement and the weapons were ordered. Now all they had to do was wait. Grandpa contacted Sheriff Perkins and filled him in on their new mission. He was glad to have some help dealing with that killer bear and promised to call them for help whenever trouble arose. Grandpa began holding daily training classes on survival skills with the grandkids. They learned tracking, navigation, food preparation, fire-starting, edible vegetation, knot tying, and building shelters and bear traps. This made the days fly by as they waited for their custom-built weapons to arrive.

CHAPTER 8

MYSTERIOUS STRANGERS

E very day the kids would run to the post office looking for their special package.

"This is worse than waiting for Christmas," complained Maddox.

"I know," agreed Taven, "When is that package ever going to get here?"

"Remember what Grandma always says, 'patience is a virtue,'" reminded Aria.

"We know, we're just running out of virtue, that's all," kidded Taven.

Several days passed when one morning while the kids were getting ready to make their daily run to the post office, Aria looked up. "Hey, who's that coming up the driveway? It looks like a mail truck."

As the stranger got closer, they recognized him as Gus Gustavson, the postmaster. Shrieks of joy filled the air as the kids ran down the lane to meet Gus.

"Well, I know you've been anxious to get this package so I figured the least I could do was bring it out to you."

They all thanked him and helped set the heavy box on the front porch.

"That was mighty nice of you, Gus," said Grandpa, as he walked around the side of the house. "Well, it finally arrived. Let's open it and see what's inside."

Grandpa took out his pocketknife and cut the packing tape. They stood in suspense as Grandpa opened the lid and reached in. A smile came over the children's faces as he passed out each item. It was even better than they had imagined. The archery equipment, the sword, shield and helmet, the knives, spears and the medical kit were all top of the line and made with precision craftsmanship.

"Now," said Grandpa, "our real work begins. Training starts tomorrow morning, right after breakfast."

The children didn't need any coaxing to be at the training site on time as it seemed more like play than work. Every day was focused on learning the special skills they would need for dealing with Single Claw. Grandpa was impressed with their fast progress as they began their lessons on self-defense and search and rescue.

About three weeks later, when the 6:15 train pulled into Sawdust Springs, two mysterious passengers stepped off onto the loading dock. Each carried a large, heavy duffel bag on his shoulder. The strangest thing about them was their clothing. They wore old, faded Confederate uniforms and they looked like they had stepped right out of the Civil War. After getting directions from the porter, they headed across town to the Caribou Hotel.

Sheriff Perkins was just finishing supper at the hotel when the two strangers entered the lobby. He couldn't help but notice their unusual clothes. His eyes followed them as they checked in at the lobby and then entered the dining room for supper. They took a table directly across from him.

"Hello men," he called over to them. "Welcome to Sawdust Springs. Let me introduce myself, I'm Sheriff Perkins." He reached over to shake their hands. There was an awkward silence as they hesitated to take his handshake. Finally, one of them extended his hand and said,

"Nice to meet you Sheriff, my name's Ben Harden and this here's my brother, Will."

"What brings you to Sawdust Springs?" asked the sheriff.

"Well, we're hoping to do a little prospecting in the streams around Bear Mountain." answered Ben. "No law against that, is there?"

"No, I guess not," replied sheriff Perkins, "It's not often we get prospectors in this neck of the woods anymore. The big rush ended over fifty years ago."

Sheriff Perkins had an uneasy feeling about these two. Something just didn't seem right. "How long do you two plan to be in the area?"

"Just a few weeks, then we'll be moving on," answered Ben.

His brother, Will, never said a word., He let Ben do all the talking.

"Before you go prospecting around Bear Mountain," said sheriff Perkins, "there's a few things you ought to know. Come on over to my office in the morning and I'll fill you in on the dangers of an old Indian legend."

"An old Indian legend?" Ben repeated, "You've got my curiosity up. We'll be there right after breakfast."

His brother, Will, shoved his sleeve up to check his watch. Sheriff Perkins happened to notice the letters "KGC" tattooed on his wrist. But before he could ask about the tattoo, Ben announced that it was getting late and said they needed to hit the hay as soon as possible. The sheriff thought it best to wait till morning before asking any more questions.

That same night, everyone sat around the table enjoying another one of Grandma's delicious home cooked dinners. The phone rang and Grandpa went to answer it.

"Hello…No, we're still up, what's on your mind, sheriff? No, I wasn't aware of any prospectors coming to town. Does seem a little unusual for prospectors showing up at Sawdust Springs, what'd they look like?… Confederate uniforms you say? … That does seem strange. Anything else you noticed?"

Grandpa became silent and a stunned look came over his face.

"A tattoo on his wrist? Are you sure the initials were 'KGC?'" Yeah, that's probably the best … wait till morning to question them….I see, well, I agree. It's a good idea with all the trouble we've been having up there. I'll ask the Bear Hunters and get back to you in the morning. Have a good evening, Sheriff."

The children were listening in on the one-sided conversation and smiled when Grandpa referred to them as the 'Bear hunters.'

"What was that all about?" asked Grandma.

Grandpa hung up the phone and sat back down at the dinner table.

"Sheriff Perkins wants us to help keep an eye on a couple of rough looking characters that just came into town. They're heading to Bear Mountain, supposedly to prospect for gold. He wants us to see if they're up to mischief and also to keep watch for Single Claw."

"Grandpa, why did you mention the initials, KGC?" asked Aria.

He explained what the Sheriff told him about the tattoo and the Confederate uniforms.

"You don't suppose some Knights of the Golden Circle have come looking for Rawhide's gold, do you?" asked Maddox.

"It sure looks that way." answered Grandpa, "What else would they be doing up here? I don't think they're really prospecting but what I can't figure out is how they knew to come to Bear Mountain."

"There must be a map somewhere showing the location of all the stashes of gold," reasoned Taven.

"Why now, after all these years would they be looking for it? The civil war's been over for years" questioned Aria. "And if they do know the location of the gold, Rawhide might be in serious trouble. We've got to warn him."

"You're right," said Grandpa, "but first we need to meet with Sheriff Perkins in the morning and find out all we can about these two characters. Remember not to let on that we know anything about the 'KGC' and the gold."

—————))⟨⟩((—————

Rawhide Jake was busy rebuilding his cabin that Single Claw had torn to pieces. Hambone was almost completely healed up from his run in with Single Claw. He spent most of his time laying around, sleeping in the shade. Conniption enjoyed scratching himself on the corral fence and eating grain while watching Rawhide work on the cabin. Rawhide had no idea his tranquil homestead was soon to be in danger from two Knights of the Golden Circle who were in the territory looking for the hidden gold. With the Confederacy completely dissolved, that was the last thing on his mind. He figured even if there were still Knights alive today, they would never be called back to the south with their precious cargo. After all, who would want to start another civil war?

—————))⟨⟩((—————

The following morning, Grandpa and the Bear Hunters waited until the strangers had left before going over to the sheriff's office.

"How'd your meeting go?" asked Grandpa, "Did you get any more information from them?"

"I think so," answered the sheriff. "They didn't seem worried at all when I told them about Single Claw. I warned them about starting a campfire. We'll soon see if they took me seriously."

Grandpa asked why they were prospecting for gold at Bear Mountain.

"I asked them that too," said sheriff Perkins. "They pulled out an old, tattered, torn map that a friend had given them and said it was supposed to lead to a vein of gold. Some of the map was missing, but what was still legible showed a trail leading to the Caribou River, winding along a rock ledge. From there, it crossed over the river on a suspension bridge and into a box canyon. That's as much as it showed because the rest of the map was missing. I reassured them that they were on a wild goose chase because there isn't anything like that around Bear Mountain. I should know, I've spent most of my life in these mountains. Someone probably had a good time fabricating a whopper like that."

The Bear Hunters did their best to show no expression, knowing what they did about the secret passage.

"What'd they do then?" asked Grandpa, "Did they give up their search and head home?"

Not at all," replied the sheriff., "They were bound and determined to believe that their map was real. They took off about an hour ago in the direction of Bear Mountain. I'd sure appreciate it if you'd follow them at a distance and see what they're up to."

"We'll be glad to," answered Grandpa, " I suspect there's a lot more to their story than they're letting on. By the way, did they say where they got the map?"

"I asked them," said the sheriff, " but they had sworn a vow of secrecy not to disclose its origin."

Grandpa reassured the sheriff that they'd be careful and not do anything but observe from a distance. After leaving the sheriff's office, Grandpa gathered the kids around him. "The fact that those two strangers had a map to the box canyon tells us they really are Knights of the Golden Circle. The dead confederate soldier back in the caves must have made a map to show the gold's location and sent it to his superiors. It's good for us that part of the map is missing. We better go back to the cabin and get our supplies and weapons. We've no time to lose.

The Harden brothers, Ben and Will made good progress the first day and set up camp just beyond Loon Lake. "What do you think about that legend the sheriff told us?" asked Will, "You know, about a bear called Single Claw and not making any campfires?"

"I don't know what to make of that." answered Ben., "He might've just wanted to scare us off, but just to be on the safe side, maybe we shouldn't make a fire tonight. I've got enough beef jerky to get us by."

"Ben, I've been thinking," said Will.

"About what?" questioned Ben.

"You know, about if we're doing the right thing or not, looking for another Knight's gold. After all, I'm the descendant in our family to be a Knight of the Golden Circle since I'm the youngest. Our family has watched over the gold faithfully all these years until you convinced me that the south was lost forever. I gave in to spending some of that gold, but now you just want to get all you can. The way I see it, it's nothing more than pure greed."

"Now don't go worrying yourself, little brother," said Ben., "Why shouldn't we have some of that treasure instead of just letting it collect dust in some old hideout?"

"Well, what about the curse on anyone that violates the oath that was taken with President Davis?" asked Will.

"Oh, that's just a bunch of superstition to keep people in line," answered Ben.

"I sure hope you're right," said Will as he crawled into his sleeping bag.

Miles away across the valley, the sound of a strange animal echoed through the darkness, a sound they had never heard before.

CHAPTER 9

NARROW ESCAPE

G randpa and the Bear Hunters quietly made their way to the top of a high ridge. There they could keep watch on the campsite of the Harden brothers far below them. It was a perfect place for surveillance. Camouflaged with leaves and twigs stuck in their hats, they were careful not to be seen.

"Don't make any sound," whispered Grandpa, "We don't want to give away our position." Just then, they heard the roar of a large bear.

"Creepers," whispered Taven, "sounds like Single Claw is on the war path again."

"Yeah," said Grandpa, "I'm sure glad they took the sheriff's advice and didn't start a campfire. Otherwise they'd be having a surprise visitor tonight."

They pulled back from view and spread out their sleeping bags. Sleeping out in the open, they enjoyed the beautiful moonlit sky filled with brilliant stars.

The next morning the two strangers woke early and cleared out of camp, heading in the direction of the secret passage.

"I sure hope they don't discover the hidden trail," said Aria.

"The bad thing is, they know it exists, so they're going to be looking extra hard for it." said Grandpa. "I only hope that map isn't very accurate when it comes to distances."

Using binoculars, they were able to follow far enough back so they wouldn't be detected. Several hours later, Ben and Will Harden were getting close to the hidden trail.

"Look here!" said Ben. "Here's the bend in the trail just like on the map. We can't be too far from it now."

The map was more specific than Grandpa had hoped it would be.

"Over here!" said Will., "Here's the large flat rock indicating where the trail is." They turned the rock over, and underneath were chiseled the letters, KGC, with an arrow pointing east.

"Yahoo!," shouted Ben., "We found it!" It didn't take but a few minutes to locate the brush pile at the start of the hidden trail.

Watching through their binoculars, our little band of detectives were disappointed at how easy the discovery was made.

"Well, that's the first clue," said Taven. "It shouldn't take them long at all to reach the box canyon."

"You're right," said Grandpa, "but that's where the map is torn and missing the clue to the cave entrance. Let's hope that's as far as they get."

Then Grandpa had an idea. "Rawhide told me of another route to his cabin that winds around the north side of the mountain. It's longer, but hopefully we can get there ahead of those two characters. We'd better hurry though, just in case they discover the secret entrance to the caves."

The race was on. Rawhide had to be warned of the advancing danger. He had once saved their lives; now it was their turn to save him.

Grandpa and the Bear Hunters took off in haste along the northern route around the mountain. "Keep your eyes peeled for a large log fallen across this creek we're following," said Grandpa, "Rawhide said it's our only clue to the trail that leads to his cabin on this side of the mountain."

It wasn't long before Aria spotted it through the underbrush. "There it is, Grandpa, just up ahead."

Crossing the log, they found that the seldom used trail was overgrown with brush and much harder to travel. Progress was a lot slower. The trail climbed along the mountain and narrowed with a steep drop-off to the river below.

"Be careful," warned Grandpa, "We better tie off. This is very dangerous. One slip and it would be all over!" After tying together with rope they safely made it past the steep canyon.

Then they heard it, the roar of Single Claw from somewhere behind them in the valley below.

"I'm sure glad he sounds far away," said Taven.

"Me too," said Aria, "Sounds like he's way down in the valley."

"That's good," said Maddox, "Let's just hope he stays that way."

It wasn't long before they came to a fork in the trail that led off in two different directions. "Rawhide didn't say anything about this," said Grandpa, "I'm not sure which one we should take."

"The one on the left looks like it's been traveled a little bit more," said Aria.

"I think you're right," agreed Grandpa, "Let's take that one."

They hadn't gone far when they heard Single Claw again. "Oh no," said Maddox, ``I think he's getting closer. You don't suppose he's following us again? Now what are we going to do?"

"First, let's stop and get your weapons ready. This time, I don't want us to be caught by surprise. Somehow, that bear must've caught our scent and decided to check us out," explained Grandpa. "Hurry, maybe we can make it to Rawhide's cabin before he catches up with us."

The narrow trail became hazardous as it wound upward along the side of the mountain. On one side were steep rock cliffs and on the other was a thousand foot drop off. The trail was just wide enough for Single Claw to follow. Every so often, a roar indicated that he was getting closer.

They were moving along as fast as they could, when they saw something that was shocking and unbelievable. Just up ahead, the trail came to a dead end. Sheer rock cliffs blocked any forward progress.

"We've taken the wrong trail," exclaimed Grandpa. "Now we're in real trouble." They were trapped on a dead end trail with no place to hide, and Single Claw was quickly closing the gap. Soon, he'd be face to face with them.

"What'll we do now?" yelled Maddox. "We haven't got a chance!"

"Calm down now;" instructed Grandpa, "remember the training you've been going through. Panic is the number one killer in situations like this. We've got to stay calm and think."

Grandpa grabbed a stick and drew a line across the trail. "We'll form a defense right here. I'll stand at the front with my rifle, andTaven, I want you to get behind me with your sword and shield. The rest of you form a line behind us." The Bear Hunters took up their positions. Then they waited for what seemed like an eternity. They could hear the bear coming closer and closer. Suddenly, Grandpa turned around.

"I've got an idea! Everyone start gathering dry grass, leaves and twigs as fast as you can."

"But why, Grandpa?" asked Taven. "What good will that do?"

"Never mind, just do as you're told," Grandpa commanded.

In a few minutes, they had handfuls of dry brush. "Quick Aria, bring me a couple of your arrows." Grandpa began tying the tender dry material to the tip of the arrows. "Now Aria, draw back your bow as far as you can and hold it until I light the tip of the arrow. Then I want you to shoot it down the canyon across the river." Aria did as Grandpa instructed and shot the flaming arrow into the valley below. They repeated the process a second time. "I get it!" said Taven, "If Single Claw catches the scent of that fire, he might go after it."

"Right," said Grandpa, "And because everything is so wet now it won't start a forest fire. Now let's see if my plan works. Take your positions again and be ready."

Single Claw was just about on them when he stopped and sniffed the air. He had caught the scent of the flaming arrows. Suddenly, he spun around and headed down the trail where he could cross the river. A rage came over him as he got closer to the smoke. "Look everybody, way down there," said an excited Maddox as he looked down the cliff, "Grandpa's plan worked. Single Claw is crossing the river trying to get to the fire."

"Now's our chance," said Grandpa. "Let's run back down the mountain and take the other trail."

The kids didn't have to be told twice as they took off running as fast as their little legs would carry them. In about twenty minutes, they reached the spot where the trail split and headed off in a different direction. This trail led through the woods, far away from the steep mountain cliffs. They traveled about two miles before Grandpa called for a rest. Once again, God had protected them from an encounter with Single Claw.

"That was a close one," said Grandpa. "I have a feeling we're going to confront that creature face to face one of these days."

"You bet, and we'll teach him a lesson he'll never forget," said Aria.

Several hours later, they came to a clearing with a log cabin in it.

"There it is," said Grandpa, "Rawhide's cabin." A few moments later, Hambone greeted them with his familiar howl. Conniption joined in baying with her loud Hee Haw's.

"Nobody's gonna sneak up on me," laughed Rawhide, as he stepped out the door. "What brings you back up my way so soon?"

While the kids greeted the animals, Grandpa explained everything to Rawhide. He told him about the two Confederate soldiers who had come into town with an old map looking for gold, and the letters "KGC" tattooed on one of their wrist. He then told him about their narrow escape from Single Claw.

"Oh, corn whiskers," said Rawhide, scratching his head. "I forgot about that fork in the trail., I'm sure glad nothing happened to you. It's hard to believe, after all these years, that the Knights have come looking for that gold. Why would the south want that gold back now? They're never going to fight another Civil war."

"Well, I don't think they were sent here by the south," said Grandpa.

"I've got a sneaky suspicion they're here on their own accord. We'll stick around to make sure everything's OK before heading back down." For the next few days, Grandpa and the Bear Hunters rolled up their sleeves and went to work. It was a perfect opportunity to give Rawhide some much needed help in putting his cabin back together.

Four days later, they were just sitting down for supper when Hambone and Conniption began announcing that a visitor was coming. Grandpa and Rawhide grabbed their rifles and stood on the front porch, looking for any intruders. "You kids stay inside just in case there's trouble," ordered Grandpa.

"Howdy friend," came a voice from down the trail. Two men dressed in normal prospecting clothes started toward the cabin.

"Don't mean any trouble, just looking for a prospector named Rawhide Jake."

"That would be me," answered Rawhide, as the two strangers moved closer to the cabin.

"What do you want from me, anyway?"

Ben Harden walked closer to the cabin, explaining that he and his brother were prospectors looking for gold and that the hotel manager back at Sawdust Springs told them the only gold mine in the area belonged to Rawhide Jake.

"That's right," grumbled Rawhide, as he pointed his gun directly at the two intruders. "Don't come any closer. Now you two best be getting on your way."

Rawhide knew a lot more about them than they did about him.

"It's getting late and we were kind of hoping we could sleep in your barn, if that's OK?" asked Ben. "We don't mean you any harm."

Rawhide knew the code of the north was to help anyone in need.

"Alright, but just for tonight; then I want you to leave." barked Rawhide. He knew those two were up to no good and he planned to keep a close eye on them. The fact that they had discovered the hidden trail was enough to make Rawhide madder than a poked stick badger. "How'd you find my cabin, anyway?" Rawhide demanded.

Ben nervously shuffled from one foot to the other while he explained that they had found an old map that led them to a secret trail. Once they were in the box canyon, they couldn't figure out where to go.

Then, one evening, they noticed bats by the thousands coming out of the side of the mountain. Their curiosity got the best of them and when they went to see where the bats were coming from, they discovered the entrance to the caves. The rest was easy, because the exit from the caves on the other side of the mountain led directly to this cabin.

Rawhide was outwardly frustrated and threw his hat on the ground.

"confound it, you two better keep this to yourselves, you hear? I don't want anyone else finding their way up here."

They shook their heads in agreement as they turned and headed out to the barn.

CHAPTER 10

DEATH ON BEAR MOUNTAIN

No one slept soundly that night, knowing that two Knights of the Golden Circle were staying out in the barn. Rawhide Jake and Grandpa were waiting to see what the two brothers' next move might be. Maybe they would just go back to where they came from, but that was doubtful. The next morning Rawhide was fixing breakfast and Grandpa, and his grandkids were rolling up their sleeping bags when all of a sudden the front door flew open. Standing in the doorway were Ben and Will Hardin, each holding a rifle aimed directly at them.

"Don't make a move!" hollered Ben. "Put your hands in the air."

"Do as they say," instructed Grandpa, "They mean business."

"You bet we do," sneered Ben., "Anyone trying anything funny will be shot."

"Why you yellow-bellied, sneaking, sorry sidewinders! I should have ran you off when I had the chance," grumbled Rawhide.

"Be quiet old man!" shouted Ben.

"Everyone sit down with your hands behind your back," ordered Will. It was the first time Will had finally spoken. He then tied their hands while Ben kept his gun on them.

"What do you plan to do with us?" asked Grandpa. "Why did you tie us up?"

"What we want to know is the location of that old codger's goldmine, that's all," snarled Ben. The brothers suspected that Rawhide's goldmine and the hidden Confederate gold were one and the same.

"I'll never tell you, you sneaking, thieving varmints!" yelled Rawhide.

At that, the two outlaws began searching high and low for any clues that might lead them to the mine. They ransacked the house but came up empty-handed. Ben found the cellar door and went downstairs. In a few minutes, he came back up holding a leather sack. "And just where did these happen to come from?" asked Ben, as he held out several coins with the inscription 'KGC' on them. I figured that was where you were getting your gold since you were the only one in the territory that had a gold mine. Now, where's the rest of it."

"You'll have to shoot me first," said Rawhide. "I'll never tell."

"You're probably right," responded Ben as he walked over to Grandpa and put the gun to his head. "Maybe this will persuade you, or don't you care if he kicks the bucket?"

"All right, all right, I'll show you but only on one condition. You let the others go and don't harm them." said a dejected Rawhide.

"You've got my word;" said Ben, "now let's get a move on."

Rawhide knew they had him over a barrel and there was nothing he could do but show them where the gold was hidden.

Rawhide led the rope-bound procession with the Harden brothers bringing up the rear. Lighting their lanterns, they entered the caves and went through the dark, winding tunnels until they came to the skeleton of the Confederate soldier. Ben and Will Harden stopped cold with eyes wide open. "Look at this ,Will!," said Ben., "It's the Knight that was guarding his stash of gold!

Turning to Rawhide, "You're doing just fine, old timer." said Ben, "now show us where he hid it."

Rawhide reluctantly went into the dead-end tunnel. He was trying to loosen the rope around his hands so he could grab a stick and fight back. The Bear Hunters saw what he was doing and were worried he'd get himself killed trying to escape.

"Rawhide," whispered Grandpa, "Don't do anything foolish. Just show them where the gold is."

"Hey! What are you two talking about?" yelled Ben.

"Nothing," answered Rawhide. "We're almost there."

Leading them down a dark tunnel, Rawhide gave the instructions,"Move this large rock away from the wall, and you'll find what you're looking for.

Ben and Will laid their guns down and excitedly rolled the rock away. They let out a rebel yell when they saw the gold. "What did I tell you?" said Ben. "We're rich!"

"We were rich before," said Will. "Now we're filthy rich! I hope this is enough gold to satisfy you?" questioned

Will. "I'm just worried that curse will come on us for what we're doing."

"Don't worry yourself, little brother, there's nothing to that curse."

They pointed their guns at their captives and ordered them to start carrying the gold out of the cave. They began tugging and dragging heavy sacks of gold outside the cave. There was so much gold that it took several hours to move it all out of the cave. Ben concentrated on keeping the prisoners guarded with his gun.

"How are we going to get all this gold down from Bear Mountain?" asked Will. "It'll take a lot of trips by ourselves."

"That's why we've got to go back to town and buy us a couple of mules," explained Ben.

"Well, what are we going to do with them while we're gone?" asked Will. "It'll take four days to make the round trip back here."

"Don't worry yourself none, I've got it all planned out." Ben told the prisoners to move back inside the cave where they couldn't be seen. Help me tie their legs so they can't get away." They bound their hostages and put gags over their mouths.

"But Ben, they'll die without any food and water."

"That's the plan," said Ben., "We can't trust them with what they know about the gold. Besides, they'll never be found inside these caves. No one will ever know what happened to them."

Will didn't like the idea of leaving them tied up. "What if they get loose and go for help? Let's finish them off quickly; that would be a lot more humane."

"You're probably right," agreed Ben., "I've got an idea." A look of evil came over him as he went over to his backpack and pulled out six sticks of dynamite. "This should do the trick," smiled Ben. "The only problem is, I don't have a fuse."

"I've got an idea," said Will., "Gather some dry grass and twigs and make a fuse trail with them. I used to do this back home on the farm when I needed a fuse to blast stumps." Will was pleased with himself for coming up with a solution about the fuse. They placed the dynamite around their prisoners and began to make a fuse trail of dry brush. The situation looked hopeless for Grandpa, Rawhide, and his Grandkids. They couldn't believe what was happening to them. How could anyone do such a wicked thing?

"Hey," said Rawhide, "I thought you agreed not to hurt us if we showed you where the gold was?"

"Well, now you know you can't trust us," sneered Ben Harden.

Grandpa bowed his head and began to pray quietly. If ever they needed a miracle, it was now.

The cruel Harden brothers were ready to carry out their evil plan.

"Here goes," said Ben as he struck a match to the fuse trail. The fire was slow to travel as some of the leaves were damp and kept wanting to go out. "I'll get some more dry twigs and leaves," said Will. After several tries, large plumes of dark smoke filled the entire area. They waited until they were sure the fire wouldn't go out again and then ran and hid behind a rock. The fuse was slowly burning towards the cave. Everything was going as planned and in a few minutes there would be no witnesses left alive. The Hardin brothers thought they had come up with the perfect crime, but they made one fatal mistake. They had started a fire on the backside of Bear Mountain!

Suddenly there was a deafening roar from a gigantic killer bear! The terrifying sound of Single Claw caught them completely by surprise. Standing on its hind legs just thirty yards away was the largest bear they had ever seen. They started to put their guns to their shoulders, but it was too late. With lightning speed, the huge bear charged out of the forest, heading straight towards the two men. It only took one second for Single Claw to be upon them. They didn't even have time to run. With one swipe of his paw, it was all over for both of them. The Harden brothers didn't have a chance. They finally reaped the fruit of their evil from a monster bear more powerful than themselves. After Single Claw finished off the greedy killers, he quickly extinguished the burning fuse by thrashing the fire to pieces. Unaware of the lives he'd just saved inside the cave, he slowly turned and lumbered back into the woods.

A sigh of relief came over everyone when they realized the fuse to the dynamite had been extinguished. Another miracle came when Taven finally managed to wiggle his hands free of the rope and in minutes untied everyone.

"Can you believe what just happened?" asked Rawhide. "I don't think I've ever been in a more hopeless situation."

"Me neither," said Grandpa. "It just goes to show you, even when there seems to be no way, God can make a way. He's a God of miracles and nothing is impossible with Him!"

"Yeah," said Taven, "who would have guessed our worst enemy, Single Claw, would be used to deliver us?"

"Grandpa?" asked Aria, "Do you think it was the curse of the gold that killed the Hardin brothers? They did betray the oath of the 'Knights of the Golden Circle'."

"No," said Grandpa, "I'd say it was the curse of greed that did them in. Greed will always bring about destruction. That's why we must never be caught up in the desire for all this gold we have. We must always use it to help others and not just for ourselves."

That evening, six grateful survivors stood next to two unmarked graves. Grandpa spoke a few words of forgiveness over the men who had tried to kill them. Maddox asked Grandpa how someone could kill innocent people for no reason?

"Well, Maddox, I don't fully understand it either, "but one thing I have learned in my life time is that hate, greed, lust, power, and murder are symptoms of something else."

"What's that?" asked Aria.

"They're symptoms of evil," said Grandpa. "There is good and evil in this world we live in, and we must never forget it. One of my favorite Bible verses that I want to live by is, "Do not be overcome by evil, but overcome evil with good."

That day, Grandpa and the Bear Hunters made a vow to fight evil whenever they could by helping people in need. Especially helping people needing rescue from the world's largest bear, Single Claw.

STORY 2

DANGER IN SAWDUST SPRINGS

CHAPTER 1

TERROR FROM BEAR MOUNTAIN

B ehind locked doors, a secret meeting was taking place in an upstairs office at Sawdust Springs. Three men were discussing a proposal that would greatly benefit one of them. Two of the men were top executives of the North Pass & Arctic Railroad company. The other was an older man wearing an expensive tailored suit. He had the appearance of a successful businessman.

"If you can get us what we want, we'll pay you $200,000 dollars," said one of the NP&A representatives.

A smile slowly crept over the older man's face, "That's a lot of money for my services, more than I've ever made in my whole life. But what you're asking me to do is next to impossible."

"Why do you think we've offered so much? If it was easy, we'd do it ourselves," snapped the short, stocky, cigar-smoking executive.

With that, the businessman walked over to the desk and signed the agreement. While shaking hands with the railroad representatives, the taller executive held on with a firm grip, "Remember, you've only got three months to deliver or the deals off."

"I remember; I'll do everything I can." As he turned and left the room, he thought to himself, "How....... how will I ever pull off this impossible task?"

⸺⸺⸺⸺》《ᴐᴐᴐ》《⸺⸺⸺⸺

An autumn storm was blowing the last leaves off the trees as the grand kids helped their grandma put together a thousand-piece jigsaw puzzle. Grandma loved working jigsaw puzzles. The old cast iron wood stove made their cabin at Sawdust Springs warm and cozy. A perfect place to be on a cold and windy night like this. The cold autumn weather comes early in the far north. Sitting in front of the crackling fire and sipping hot chocolate, Aria, Taven and Maddox considered themselves the luckiest grandkids in the whole world. For years, they had spent the summers with their grandparents at Sawdust Springs, and then return home to the big city when school started. But now, things are going to be different. Sawdust Springs was going to be their permanent home. Choosing to move to the far north was the best decision their parents had ever made. As soon as their house sold back in the city, Mom and Dad were coming north to buy the General Store from Cletus Edwards and fulfill their dreams of owning their own business. It wasn't hard to leave the hectic pace of big city life for the peace and quiet that Sawdust Springs offered. This year, the kids remained with Grandma and Grandpa after summer was over and enrolled in the local, one room country school. That way they wouldn't have to change schools in the middle of the year.

The fire was burning low, and they were just about to call it a day when they heard a loud knock on the front door.

"Who in the world could that be on a night like this?" asked a startled Grandma. Grandpa cautiously opened the door and was surprised to see a soaking wet Sheriff Perkins shivering in the doorway.

"Why, Sheriff Perkins, what brings you out on such a stormy night?" asked Grandpa. "Come on in and get out of this storm."

"Tried to phone you but the lines were dead. Must be a tree blown down somewhere," answered the Sheriff.

Grandpa placed a chair by the fire and poured a large cup of hot chocolate. "Here, this will warm you up. Now what's so important that it couldn't wait until morning?" asked Grandpa.

"We've got trouble in the town, big trouble. You were the best ones I could count on for help when I learned of the destruction a couple hours ago."

"What kind of trouble?" asked Aria. "How can we help?"

"Well, last night," continued the Sheriff, "A bear broke into Sam Benson's house and completely destroyed it. And from the looks of it, it might have been Single Claw!"

"Single Claw!" gasped Grandpa, "What makes you think it was him?"

"From the claw marks on the walls. There's only one bear that leaves a single claw mark like what I saw over at Sam's house. I'm afraid when the town folks hear about this, there's going to be a panic. No one's safe with Single

Claw on the prowl. That's why I need your help on figuring out what to do next."

"What about Sam?" asked Taven, "Is he alright?"

"Yeah," answered the Sheriff, "fortunately for him, he was spending the night at Pleasantville with his brother. Otherwise, we'd have had a real tragedy on our hands."

Grandpa told Sheriff Perkins that he'd like to bring his grandkids over to Sam's house in the morning and look for clues as to why this happened.

"It just doesn't make sense," said Grandpa, "If Sam was gone, then there wouldn't have been a fire in the stove and that's the main reason Single Claw would have torn up his house. Besides, there were a lot of other houses with wood stoves burning last night. So why weren't they attacked? This is really bad news. That bear has never come to this side of Bear Mountain. Why in the world would he start now?"

The kids were glad that the next day was Saturday and there was no school. They loved solving mysteries, and this had the makings of being a really good one.

"I want you to bring your detective kits tomorrow," Instructed Grandpa. "I want us to go over every inch of that house and look for clues as to why this happened."

The next morning, right after breakfast, they all headed over to the scene of the attack. The first thing they saw when they got close to the house was the front door laying on the porch. It had been torn clear off its hinges. Inside the house, there was no question that a bear was responsible for this. Claw marks were everywhere.

"Look at this mess!" said Maddox, "Looks just like Rawhide Jake's cabin after Single Claw tore it to pieces."

Throughout the house there was evidence that a large, powerful animal had done the damage. The stair railings were ripped off, the piano smashed, the heavy furniture was broken and thrown around like toothpicks.

"Wow, look up there," pointed William, "at those single claw marks high up the wall."

"Sure looks like Single Claw did this," said Aria.

Grandpa agreed, then instructed them about gathering evidence. He had them measure the size of the bear tracks and the length of its claws, check for food that might have been left out, and take the temperature of the ashes in the wood stove to determine when the fire had gone cold.

"Why are we doing all this?" asked Maddox, "We know it was Single Claw. Don't we?"

"A thorough detective never assumes anything, Maddox. We must let the clues speak for themselves," answered Grandpa.

It was just after noon when they completed their investigation and gathered back home to go over their evidence.

"Hopefully," said Grandpa, " we'll figure out why Single Claw invaded Sawdust Springs. You go first Taven, what did the tracks look like?"

"Well, one thing's for sure, they were definitely bear tracks. The only thing I noticed was that they seemed smaller than Single Claw's, but there was the unmistakable single claw mark on the walls."

"Yeah, I noticed that too," said Grandpa. "What about you, Aria? What did you discover?"

"Well, the one thing that seemed a little strange was the amount of food scattered throughout the house. There were small pieces of blueberry pie thrown everywhere. Sam might have made some pies and left them out on the counter"

"Maddox, could you determine how long the stove had been out?"

"My temperature probe indicated the ashes were stone cold. The fire must have been out for at least 24 hours. That means there wouldn't have been any smoke at the time of the attack to attract Single Claw."

"Do these clues help any?" asked Aria.

"Right now they don't give us very much." said Grandpa. "They raise more questions than answers."

———————⟩⟨⊃⊂⟩⟨———————

It wasn't long before the news leaked out. As hard as Sheriff Perkins tried to keep the people calm, panic began to spread, and a worried look was on everyone's face when they learned there had been a bear attack by Single Claw. The fear that he would attack again paralyzed the whole town. Men were carrying hunting rifles everywhere they went. Women and children stayed out of sight behind locked doors. There was talk about shutting down the school until the problem was resolved. Sheriff Perkins was going to call a special town meeting, hoping to squelch the growing fear. Some were even talking of moving if Single Claw wasn't stopped.

The hardest hit of all was Sam Benson. When he came back and found his home torn to pieces, he was filled with grief and despair. Being in his seventies, Sam didn't have the strength or finances to repair the extensive damage. His mortgage was to be paid off in three more years. There was no way he could afford to pay for the repairs and still make his house payments. The only thing he could do was put his house up for sale, what was left of it. His lot was worth more now that his house.

The next day, Sam went down to the First Northern Bank of Sawdust Springs to explain his situation to Elmer Carlson, the bank manager.

"Hello Mr. Carlson," greeted Sam as he was escorted into Mr. Carlson's office, "I suppose you've heard what happened to my house."

"Well, yes I have," answered Elmer, "I think every-body in three counties has heard by now, the way news travels. Sure, sorry to hear about your loss., What can I do to help? Do you need a loan to repair the damage?"

"Well, that's just it," said Sam., "I can't afford to take out another loan and still make my mortgage payments. The only thing left to do is sell everything. The house isn't worth much in the condition it's in, but the lot should be worth something. I just wanted to let you know what my plans are. I'll keep up the payments until it's sold."

Elmer hung his head in grief and said nothing. Finally, after a few minutes, he asked Sam how much money he planned to sell it for.

"About twenty thousand," said Sam., "That's enough to pay off my loan and leave me with a little nest egg."

"You know," said the bank manager, "the way worry is spreading like wildfire, houses are going to be pretty hard to sell. They're wanting to move out over fear of Single Claw. I'll tell you what I can do though, out of the goodness of my heart, I'll give you ten thousand dollars for your place, 'cash on the barrelhead. It'll probably cost more to fix up your old house than it's worth."

"But Mr. Carlson, that's only half of what I was hoping to get," said a dejected Sam.

"I know," said Elmer., "I wish I could pay more but that's all I can afford. That will pay off your mortgage and still leave you with a little. You think about it, there's no need to make a rush decision."

Sam was quiet for a few minutes before he spoke, "I guess you're right, selling a house in Sawdust Springs right now is probably next to impossible. I'd be crazy not to take your offer. I sure appreciate what you're trying to do for me, Mr Carlson."

"Don't think anything of it. I'll have the paperwork drawn up in the morning."

CHAPTER 2

PANIC

A heavy fog of fear was drifting down on the once tranquil and peaceful town of Sawdust Springs. Everyone was talking about Single Claw and what should be done to protect the town.

"I'll tell you what I'm going to do," said Scarface Sam., "I'm going to move to Pleasantville. Surviving one attack from that bear is enough for me.

"Maybe he's right," said one of the townspeople, "maybe we all should be thinking about moving. After all, if anyone knows the horror of that bear it's Scarface Sam." Sam had miraculously lived through an attack several years ago that left his face scarred beyond recognition. Panic and fear kept spreading like an epidemic throughout Sawdust Springs.

Back at the cabin, the grandchildren had sad faces while they went about their daily chores.

"What's the matter?" asked Grandpa,

"You look like you've just lost your best friend."

"In a way, we have," answered Aria, "We're losing Sawdust Springs. If this trouble with Single Claw isn't stopped, this place will become a ghost town. Then Mom and Dad won't move up here to buy the general store from Cletus Edwards, and that means we'll be moving back to the city."

"Now hold on," consoled Grandpa., "Don't go worrying yourself about what might happen in the future. Our responsibility is to take one day at a time, doing all we can while leaving the future in God's hands. Remember, the Bible says, 'God has not given us a spirit of fear but of power, love and a sound mind." Worrying about the "what if's" in life has never helped anyone. Let's go to the next town meeting and see what we can do to help. This thing isn't over yet." Grandpa's encouragement had given them a sliver of hope.

That same morning, the Mayor, Bud Morgan walked into Sheriff Perkins' office. "Sheriff," he said, "we've got to do something. The talk all around town is about moving to Pleasantville. If that happens, the town's going to die. We can't let one bear destroy what we've worked so hard for. We'd better call that town meeting you've been wanting tomorrow night at the community hall."

"All right mayor," said the Sheriff, "I'll do all I can to calm their fears."

The mayor instructed the sheriff to set up tight security, a twenty-four-hour surveillance on the town just in case Single Claw decided to come back. Not having any deputies, Sheriff Perkins needed help. He knew he could rely on his old friend, Grandpa, called Buck by the townspeople, and his grandkids. He told them about the round the clock security the mayor requested and asked if they would do the night shift. That being the most dangerous.

As expected, they eagerly volunteered and would start right after the town meeting tomorrow night.

That gathering of the citizens of Sawdust Springs was probably the most important meeting Sawdust Springs had ever had. The whole town showed up, a standing room only crowd. Mayor Morgan's gavel rapped on the podium, calling the meeting to order. The crowd grew silent, and all eyes turned to the Mayor. "Friends, I don't have to tell you how important this meeting is tonight." began Mayor Morgan. "We're faced with a situation that could turn Sawdust Springs into a ghost town if we don't do the right thing and do it quickly." "And what would that be?" yelled someone from the crowd. "Stay here and be killed by that bear?"

Like a chain reaction, others joined in with criticism.

"How will we survive?"

"Why can't we kill that bear?"

"Who's going to protect us?"

"We need help or we're going to move!"

"Calm down now. Get a grip on yourself." commanded the Mayor. "Remember the cholera epidemic that was sweeping the country years ago and how the whole world was in a panic. No one moved away then. We all rolled up our sleeves and helped each other. Caring for the sick, cutting firewood for needy families, cooking meals, scrubbing floors and setting up a makeshift hospital. We showed bravery and courage as we trusted God to help us. Well, this is just like that pandemic. We need to balance bravery with caution as we face this new challenge to our community.

At that, Grandpa stepped up to the podium. "I'll help, along with my wife and grandkids. Since the school has closed, we can watch the town every night until this crisis is passed. We're not afraid of Single Claw. We've had four encounters with him and we're standing here tonight alive and well. Single Claw can be beat and we're willing to do all we can to see that happen. What we need is your confidence and trust until our job is done." The crowd knew that if an aged grandfather and his family were willing to risk their lives for them, the least they could do was give them a chance to do something about that bear. The tension calmed and after Sheriff Perkins' gave a few closing comments, they adjourned.

"OK," said Grandpa, "let's go home and get our weapons. We've got an important job to do, and we can't let the townspeople down."

"We sure do," said Aria. "Mom and dad won't move up here and buy the general store if Sawdust Springs becomes a ghost town."

"Grandpa, do you think we should stay together or split up?" asked Taven.

"No, I think it would be best to stay together. Let's go to the north end of town where the attack took place and begin our stake out."

The night was dark and windy. An owl hooted from the church steeple while an orchestra of dogs barked their wailing symphony throughout the deserted streets. The eerie clouds drifting by the full moon reminded the kids that Halloween was only four days away.

"Wow," said Maddox, "this sure is a creepy night. Especially since we're waiting for Single Claw, the largest bear in the world, to show up."

"What will we do if he does come?" asked Taven.

"Make a lot of commotion and try to scare him out of town!" answered Grandpa. "We don't want a direct confrontation if it can be avoided."

"Maybe Single Claw's not coming back," said Aria.

"Well, let's hope so," said Grandpa., "That would put everybody at ease."

The cold night passed without incident. Except for an occasional cat fight, everything seemed normal. They headed back to their cabin for some much-needed rest. The day passed quickly and while they were getting ready for another night of security watch there was a loud knock on the door. When Aria opened it, she was greeted by their old buddy, Rufus. Rufus was a special friend they had taken under their wings. He was 6' 4" tall and weighed 250 lbs. His large stature matched the size of his heart. He would do anything in the world for his friends, or anyone for that matter. Although he was 24 years old, his mind had stopped developing when he was around 10 years of age. He would forever be a gentle little boy who loved to play games and hang out with the grandkids.

"Hoi," said Rufus., "Whoat you upt to." Rufus talked with an accent that everybody in town recognized.

"We're just leaving for another night of guard duty on the town. We're keeping an eye out for Single Claw," said Grandpa. "Oh booy," said Rufus, "can oi come tue?"

"Maybe for a little while," said Grandpa, "but you can't stay the whole night. Your brother Jed would be worried sick over you." Jed was much older that Rufus and had taken care of him ever since their parents had died.

"Geee, tanks, this will be exciting," said Rufus.

Rufus tagged along, happy to be part of such an important job.

Grandpa instructed everyone where to take up their positions so they wouldn't be seen. Rufus was stationed with Maddox behind a large cedar tree and told to keep a lookout for anything that looked suspicious. He took his job so serious that nothing could move without him noticing it, not even a leaf blowing across the street. After a couple of hours, Grandpa thanked Rufus and told him he'd better head home before his brother started worrying about him.

"Oky, doky," said Rufus, Oi sure had fun tonight." Tanks for letting me help save the town."

"It was our pleasure," said Grandpa. "Thank you for being such a good helper." Rufus smiled with delight as he headed towards home.

Their second night turned out to be as non-eventful as the first. No sight or sound of anything coming into town. The townspeople were starting to calm down a bit and their panic was subsiding. Everyone was grateful to Grandpa and the Bear Hunters for guarding their town.

CHAPTER 3

FALSE SECURITY

Single Claw hadn't come back for two days now, bringing a sigh of relief to everyone. The last couple nights had been quiet, and everyone was beginning to feel more secure. Still, Grandpa didn't have a good feeling about the whole situation. Something just didn't seem right. Why would Single Claw come to Sawdust Springs and destroy a house that wasn't even using a wood stove? Fire was always the main thing that drove that bear into a rage. It just didn't add up.

The third night started out quiet and calm. "I think we should keep our positions on the north end of town," said Grandpa. "That's the closest to Bear Mountain and where the only attack took place."

"I agree," said Aria. "That's the most likely place for Single Claw to enter town."

The autumn wind made the trees sway in the darkness, creating the perfect mood for the night before Halloween.

"Jumping horny toads!" exclaimed Maddox, "I just realized tomorrow night is Halloween and I don't even have my costume picked out!"

"Me neither," said Taven, "I want to go as a cowboy, how about you?" Maddox thought for a minute, "I think I'll go as a puppy. What are you going to be Aria?"

"I'm going to be an Indian Princess and I volunteered to help out at the community hall with the apple bobbing contest.

"Can we get tomorrow night off?" asked Aria, "because it's Halloween and everything's been so quiet. We've not seen a sign of any bear."

"I suppose," said Grandpa, "but only if tonight goes as good as the last two."

The town clock struck midnight as Grandpa and the Bear Hunters checked the back yards and alleyways of Sawdust Springs, looking for Single Claw. Then from across town, they heard a truck coming at breakneck speed. Elmer Carlson, the banker, came driving up faster than a hound in a fox hunt. He slid his pickup truck to a stop in a cloud of dust.

"What's the matter Elmer, are you OK?" asked Grandpa.

"I...I think I just saw Single Claw," said the wide-eyed banker.

"Where did you see him?"

"On the south end of town. I was driving past the City Park when I'm sure I saw a large bear lurking in the shadows behind widow Martins' house."

"That's bad!" said Grandpa, "Widow Martin lives all alone. Elmer, take us down there in your pickup, we've no time to lose. Hurry kids, jump in the back of his truck."

Elmer raced back across town and dropped them off where he'd seen the bear. "Right over there," he pointed to the dark driveway behind the widow's house. "If it's all the same to you, I think I'll take off, this makes me awfully nervous."

"Sure," said Grandpa, "we'll handle it from here." Grandpa turned and gave instructions. "Aria, you check the side yard. Taven and Maddox, come with me. Be sure and signal with your owl call if you see anything."

Grandpa took off toward the back of widow Martin's house. Everyone's heart was beating hard, and the suspense was mounting. At any moment the largest bear in the world could attack them from the darkness. In spite of a full moon, dark shadows were everywhere. And every dark shadow seemed to conceal a crouching bear. Their imaginations were running wild. They all breathed a sigh of relief when they met up in the side yard.

"It's too quiet for Single Claw to be around here," said Aria. "I haven't seen or heard anything, not even a twig snap."

"We didn't either," said Grandpa. "Maybe Elmer's imagination was playing tricks on him. Just to be on the safe side, we better stick around and make sure there's no bear at this end of town."

The sunrise had a special warmth after the long, cold, autumn night. The grand kids were holding up well under such a strenuous schedule but now they sure could use a hot breakfast and some sleep.

"Let's head home," said Grandpa, "We've had another uneventful but successful night."

The road to their cabin ran right by Sam Benson's house that Single Claw had destroyed. As the tired, groggy kids walked by Sam's house, no one noticed his neighbor, Jake Taylor's place. They were just about past when something caught Taven's eye. "Wow, will you look at that!" he hollered. Everyone stopped, wondering what Taven had seen. When they looked up, their mouths dropped wide open with surprise.

"Look," said Aria, "the porch railing is knocked down and the front door is wide open. You don't suppose...?" Grandpa nodded as he ran over to look for Jake. "Jake!" yelled Grandpa, "are you in there? Are you OK?"

There was no answer.

When they entered through the broken door, they saw the same kind of destruction that tore up Sam Benson's house. The place was a total shamble. Single Claw had left his signature claw marks everywhere. They quickly went through every room, looking for Jake but he wasn't there.

"I can't believe this!" said Grandpa., "While we were at the other end of town, we had another bear attack. Sawdust Springs wasn't as secure as we thought it was. Let's go home and call Sheriff Perkins. We need to get our detective kits out again and go over this crime scene in the morning."

Sheriff Perkins arrived at the log cabin and Grandma poured him a hot cup of coffee. A look of despair was on everyone's face. Grandpa explained why they were at the other end of town when the bear attack took place.

"If that doesn't beat all.," said Grandpa. "The only time we left the north end, Single Claw came."

Sheriff Perkins was concerned over the reaction of the townspeople. "They're really going to panic now," said the sheriff., "I don't know what we're going to do. One good thing, Jake was out of town delivering lumber. We've been fortunate so far not to have any casualties."

"The first thing I'm going to do is look for clues," said Grandpa, "There's something fishy about all this that just doesn't make sense."

Right after breakfast, Grandpa and the Bear Hunters went back to Jake's house and began gathering evidence.

CHAPTER 4

THE STAKE OUT

Elmer Carlson, the town's banker, was waiting at Jake Taylor's house when he came back from his lumber delivery that afternoon. Jake had been a bachelor all his life and, just like his neighbor Sam, the only thing he had was his house and property. He'd sworn never to sell it as long as he lived. The shock of seeing it vandalized was almost more than he could bear. Elmer consoled Jake over his loss.

"You know, Jake," began Elmer, "I'm awfully sorry about your house. I know it was the only thing you had in the whole world. I wish there was something I could do to help."

"Thanks, Mr. Carlson," said Jake., "I don't know what I'm going to do now. Built this place with my own hands; now it's totally worthless. After this second attack, the whole town will probably move to Pleasantville. I couldn't sell it if I wanted."

"I'll tell you what I'll do," said Elmer, "Just to help you out, I'll give you ten thousand dollars for your broken-down home. I did the same for your neighbor, Sam, and the least I can do is help you out as well."

"That's mighty kind of you," said Jake. "I'm sure I'll take your offer; just give me a day or two to think about it."

"No problem," smiled the banker., "I'll draw up the papers and be ready whenever you want to close the deal."

The townspeople heard about the generous offer Elmer had made and thought mighty highly of him.

Grandpa and the Bear Hunters gathered in the kitchen to go over the evidence they'd collected. The discoveries were the same as they had been in the first attack but now, they made a lot more sense. "I 'm beginning to see a connection between these two bear attacks," said Grandpa.

"See what?" asked Maddox.

"The similarity of these attacks." First, we know that Single Claw only goes into his murderous rage when he smells fire. In both cases, there was no fire in their stoves. Second, the tracks were smaller than the ones we've seen before of Single Claw's. Third, blueberry pie was scattered around inside the house. And fourth, the occupant of both houses was gone when the bear came. Both attacks were identical. ``

"What does that mean?" asked Taven.

"Well, it looks to me like someone set this up. It's not just a random bear attack."

"Why would anyone do something like that?" asked Aria, "and what does it all mean?"

"I don't know the motive, but that's what we need to find out".

"So, you think it wasn't Single Claw?" Asked Maddox.

"That's right," said Grandpa, "I don't think it was him. The blueberry pie at both places is what really tipped me off."

"What would that mean?" asked Aria.

"I can't be 100% sure," said Grandpa, "but do you remember the old television show, *Grizzly Adams*, about a large grizzly bear named Gentle Ben. About thirty years ago, I met one of the bear trainers that worked on that show. I asked him how they got the bear to attack a log cabin so ferociously. He said it was easy, all they had to do was smear blueberry pies inside the cabin and the bear would go nuts trying to get in. Bears just love blueberry pie. They dubbed in the growling sounds to make it look real. I'm willing to bet that's how someone is getting a trained bear to break into those houses. And it's no coincidence that no one's home when the attack comes. That way, the house can be smeared with the pies ahead of time. If we only knew where the next attack will be, we could be there waiting for them."

"I've got an idea.," said Aria, "Let's call Sheriff Perkins and see if he knows of anyone who is going to be out of town, leaving an empty house."

"Great idea," said Grandpa. "That's one of the common denominators in each attack."

They phoned the sheriff, and he said the only person he knew that was out of town was Cliff Edwards, who was on vacation.

"Cliff Edwards!" exclaimed Grandpa.

"That's right.," replied the sheriff., "Why does that surprise you?"

"Well, Cliff Edwards is right next door to Jake and Sam's. If my suspicions are right, someone is wanting the property that those houses sit on. I'll be right down, Sheriff, and explain what we've discovered."

When the two men looked at a map of Sawdust Springs, it was clear that those three houses sat right in the middle of the route to Bear Mountain. The question was, why would someone want access to Bear Mountain?

"Tonight, we'll get the jump on that bear that's doing all the destruction," said Grandpa.

"How are we going to do that?" asked Taven.

Grandpa explained that they should have a stake out at Cliff Edwards' house tonight. "We'll meet after it gets dark and set up our positions inside the house. If any bear comes, we'll be there waiting."

"But Grandpa," interrupted Maddox, "tonight is Halloween!"

"I know," said Grandpa, "but this is far more important. This might even save the town of Sawdust Springs if we can solve this mystery."

The kids knew he was right but were disappointed. "Sometimes in life we have to put our own desires aside in order to help others," explained Grandpa.

It would be hard to miss the big party, but they knew Grandpa was right and agreed to meet at Cliff's house right after sundown.

It was a perfect Halloween night. Just like the last three had been. Off in the distance, the haunting howl of a lone wolf was heard. Wind-swept leaves raced through the town. The full moon gave its same eerie light that danced with the shadows of the swaying trees. A barn owl began to hoot. What a night for trick or treating! Unfortunately, there would be no trick or treating in Sawdust Springs on this Halloween. With a killer bear on the loose, the town was celebrating Halloween at the Community Center to keep the kids off the streets.

Grandpa and the Bear Hunters silently made their way to the backyard of Cliff Edwards' house. Keeping in the shadows, they were careful not to be seen. They were all well-prepared, with their weapons ready. Taven had his sword, shield and helmet, Aria had her bow and arrows, and Maddox carried his throwing knives and spear. Grandpa was the main support with his lever-action rifle. The Bear Hunters had trained for months for such a time as this. Tonight, might give them the opportunity to test just how ready they were. Grandpa took a crowbar and pried open a back bedroom window. One by one, they quietly climbed in through the open window and waited for instructions.

"OK," said Grandpa, "we're in. Taven, I want you to take your position by the piano. Aria, you hide behind the couch, and Maddox, get behind the curtains. I'll crouch down under this coffee table. If any bear tries to break in here tonight, he'll find the surprise of his life."

"Grandpa," said Aria, "Do you smell that? It's blueberry pie."

"It sure is," answered Grandpa. Taking his flashlight, they could see that someone had taken blueberry pies and smeared them throughout the house.

"Your suspicions were right," said Taven. "Someone's came here earlier and baited the house with pies."

Now they knew for sure they were in the right house and that the next attack would be tonight.

CHAPTER 5

SURPRISE VISITOR

C liff Edwards wasn't due back from his vacation for another week. No one knew that he'd decided to come home early. When he pulled into Sawdust Springs around seven o'clock, he noticed that the streets were empty, and the town seemed awfully quiet. Cliff didn't have a clue that his place was the next target for destruction and that four-armed people were inside his house waiting for a killer bear to arrive. The thought that he might be mistaken for an intruder in his own house never crossed his mind.

Across town, Sheriff Perkins locked up his office before heading over to the community hall in his squad car to check out the Halloween celebrations. When he turned on Main Street, he passed an old pickup truck. He glanced in his rear-view mirror and couldn't believe who the driver was–Cliff Edwards! "Oh no," thought Sheriff Perkins, "what's he doing back in town a week early?" Cliff had to be stopped before he got to his house. The sheriff made a U-turn and flipped on his lights and siren. In a few moments Mr. Edwards was pulled over and informed about everything. He was very under-standing, and the Sheriff took him back to his station to spend the night.

Several hours went by and our stake-out crew was getting restless.

"Boy, it sure is quiet tonight." whispered Aria.

"I know," said Taven, "I'm starting to get sleepy."

"Stay alert now," encouraged Grandpa, "Our sur-prise visitor could come at any moment." The words had barely left his mouth when they heard something coming towards the house. Everyone tensed up as the sound came closer. The creaking of the wooden porch told them it was big and heavy. Grandpa's heart was pounding as he aimed his rifle at the front door. Through the window they saw a large bear, over six feet tall, standing up on his hind legs. Any second now, the creature would burst through the door. All nerves were on high alert as they waited for the bear to attack. Then they heard something that completely confused them.

"Knock, Knock, Knock, Twick or Tweat, smell my feet, give me someting good to eat."

"What in the world?" said Grandpa. "That sounds like Rufus!"

When they cautiously opened the door, there stood Rufus in a bear costume.

"Twick or Tweat," he repeated.

"Rufus, what are you doing out here in a bear cos-tume?" asked Maddox. "Don't you know you could have been shot with all the trouble the town's been having with Single Claw?"

"Well, I sought dat's why a bear costume would be so scary. After all, it is Halloween."

"Yes, I suppose it is," said Grandpa. "You better come in with us before someone takes a pot shot at you." They explained why they were there and told Rufus he could wait with them if he hid behind the couch and didn't make any noise.

Several more hours went by, and all was quiet. Then they heard a truck pull up in front of the house. Grandpa peered out through the curtains and was surprised at what he saw.

"Who is it Grandpa?" whispered Aria.

"I don't know. It's an old pickup truck towing a horse trailer. The driver is getting out and going to the back of the trailer. It's too dark to tell who it is."

When the mysterious visitor opened the horse trailer, Grandpa couldn't believe what he saw.

"What is it? What do you see now?" asked Maddox as he watched Grandpa's surprised expression.

"Whoever it is, he's leading a large bear out of the horse trailer and pointing him towards the house." Then Grandpa saw the bear stand on his hind legs, sniff in the air and charge towards the house. Grandpa signaled for everyone to get down and take their positions. The bear sniffed and clawed at the front door. The more he smelled the blueberry pies, the more excited he got. Then, with one swipe of his huge paw, the front door crashed in. The excited bear lunged into the house, growling and snapping his teeth, looking for the blueberry pies. It was all happening faster than you can think. Grandpa quickly swung his rifle towards the bear and was just getting ready to shoot when something happened that is hard to explain. All of a sudden, the bear stopped dead in his tracks, and if ever a bear could smile, that bear did. His growls turned to soft, affectionate whimpers when he saw Rufus lift his head to see what was happening. He curiously ambled over to get a better look at the other bear hiding behind the couch. Rufus began to crawl further away, not sure of what the bear was going to do. Grandpa aimed his gun, ready to shoot, if need be, but he sensed that Rufus wasn't in any real danger. Faster than a blink of an eye, the bear reached down and scooped Rufus up in his arms. Rufus let out a squeal of fright and shouted,

"Shoot, shoot, dat's bear got me." Grandpa couldn't shoot if he wanted to for fear of hitting Rufus. Everyone had a panicked look on their faces until they realized what was happening. The bear wasn't hurting Rufus, he was giving him hugs, real bear hugs! Rufus froze with fright as the bear caressed him with hugs and licked his face. "Hey, somebody do someting," pleaded Rufus.

"It's all right Rufus, I think that trained bear just found a long-lost friend," said Grandpa, "He's just giving you bear hugs and kisses. Just stay calm and be his friend while I go check on our visitor out in the truck."

"Hey Rufus," said Taven, "I didn't know you were so good looking." With that, the kids burst out with uncontrollable laughter.

After catching his breath, Maddox said, "Jumping horny toads, Rufus, you've saved the day! You're our hero! You've made this Halloween a night we'll never forget!"

Grandpa slipped outside and quietly crept up to the driver's side of the pickup and pointed his rifle at the stranger. I don't know who was more surprised, Grandpa or the "stranger."

"Elmer Carlson! What are you doing here?" The last person Grandpa expected to find was the town banker. "I think we better go down to Sheriff Perkins office. You've got a lot of explaining to do."

Everyone loaded up in Elmer's pickup truck and headed to the Sheriff's office. Grandpa drove while Elmer sat in the passenger's seat with his head held low. The Bear Hunters rode in the back of the truck, but Rufus decided to ride in the horse trailer with his new found friend, just to keep him happy. He'd never had so many bear hugs in all his life. It was a good half hour before they could get that bear to exchange Rufus for some blueberry pie.

Elmer Carlson confessed to everything, how he was offered $200,000 if he could get the 'right-of-way' through Sawdust Springs for the North Pass & Arctic Railroad. He con-cocked this devious plan so he could get the property they needed and get all that money. It was all his idea to buy that trained movie bear and fool the town into believing it was Single Claw. He showed them how he made the single claw marks with a claw attached to a long pole. He said he never wanted to hurt anybody, that's why he always waited until no one was at home.

"I'm afraid you're going to have a long time to think about this behind bars when the judge gets through with you," said Sheriff Perkins. "You had everyone believing you were kind and benevolent by helping those people out with their mortgages when all along it was you who was causing all the trouble. You almost caused Sawdust Springs to become a ghost town!"

The townspeople were in disbelief when they heard what had happened. How could the respected town banker cause such fear and panic?

"Grandpa, how could someone do such a selfish, mean thing?" asked Aria.

"It is hard to understand. The Bible says that the love of money is the root of all kinds of evil. I think we've just witnessed that firsthand."

To thank Grandpa and the Bear Hunters, the Mayor decided to hold the biggest celebration Sawdust Springs had ever seen. A banner was hung across main street that read, "Thank you, Buck, Aria, Taven, Maddox and Rufus, our hero's for saving the town!" Everyone turned out for a huge banquet at the community center to celebrate our guests of honor.

Elmer Carlson had to pay for the restoration of the houses he had destroyed besides receiving a 20-year prison sentence.

The trained movie bear was returned to the studios and every so often, Rufus would put on his bear costume and visit his newfound friend. They both had the best times of their lives.

STORY 3

DEADLY RESCUE

CHAPTER 1

CRASH LANDING

In the far north, at the little town of Sawdust Springs, Grandpa and his three grandkids, Aria, Taven, and Maddox were picking up a load of hay for their horses. They were using the crickedy horse drawn wagon which could haul four times as much as the old pickup. They had just left Emery's Livery Stable when the roar of a plane caught everyone's attention. It passed high over the town with a sputtering noise indicating some real trouble.

"That plane sounds like it's going to crash, Grandpa," said Aria.

"It sure does," It'll take a miracle to make it over Bear Mountain the way that engine's sounding."

In a few minutes the plane was out of sight as the staccato sound faded from the sky.

"I wonder who that was?" asked Taven.

"I don't know," answered Grandpa, "but I sure hope they don't crash.

They were just about to head home when Sheriff Perkins came running down the street towards 'Buck', Grandpa's nickname.

"Buck, hold up a minute. I just got an emergency transmission call from the plane that flew over a few minutes ago. They said their engine was acting up, but they were going to try and make it over Bear Mountain. If they couldn't make an emergency landing!"

"Emergency landing!" exclaimed Grandpa. "They were headed toward the back side of Bear Mountain. That's some of the most rugged country in the world. If they go down up there, it'll be a crash landing for sure."

"My feelings exactly." agreed the Sheriff.

" Do you know who they are?" asked Aria.

"Yes, it was a government plane transporting two prisoners from the Lone Pine Correctional Institute over on Indian island," said Sheriff Perkins.

"There's four on board, the pilot, the guard, and two prisoners. Grandpa, I've got a favor to ask you. Would you and your grandkids go on a search and rescue mission if we get an emergency locator beacon, indicating they've crashed?"

"You bet," said Grandpa. "Let us know as soon as you hear something."

"But there's one thing you should know." continued the sheriff.

"Inmates from the Lone Pine prison are considered some of the hardest criminals in the country. Do you still want to go?"

After pausing a moment. "We'll still go," said Grandpa. "After all, they'll need help just like we would if we crashed up in those mountains."

They hurried home and got their chores done just in case Sheriff Perkins needed them. Sure enough, several hours later he called and said a locator beacon had been picked up on their emergency radio indicating they had gone down. Probably on the back side of Bear Mountain. He knew there was no one better to send than Buck and his grandkids to search Bear Mountain. They not only knew the territory, but also knew how to survive against the largest and most dangerous bear in the world, the great grizzly known as Single Claw. The backside of Bear Mountain was home to this awesome creature. As their reputation grew for saving people from this killer bear, they had become known throughout the far north as, "The Bear Hunters."

High in the mountains of Bear Mountain, the remains of a Cessna 4/11 were scattered over an area the size of a football field.

The tail section of the crashed plane was hanging high in the trees. Both wings were ripped off and thrown down a steep canyon. The fuselage was a mangled piece of wreckage broken in three pieces. The section that held the passengers was hanging precariously over the edge of a 1,000-foot cliff. No sign of life could be seen. It would take a miracle for anyone to survive such a terrible crash. About an hour had passed when inside the torn up, scrap of fuselage, one of the passengers began to stir. Someone was alive! Slowly the man became conscious and began checking out the other passengers. He could find only two passengers and they were both dead. After finding no survivors he began struggling to get out of the plane.

He knew that if he didn't find some blankets and start a fire, he would freeze to death at that high altitude. He had trouble moving his right leg. It didn't seem broken but was badly bruised and swollen. Finally, after much struggle, the injured man crawled out of the plane and was able to start a fire with a safety flare.

"At least I won't freeze to death" He thought to himself. That's when he spotted the third passenger lying in some bushes where he'd been thrown from the plane. The man was unconscious but still alive. Why he didn't drag him over by the fire was a mystery.

———————))◄③○►((———————

Back at Sawdust Springs, Sheriff Perkins had gotten another call from the prison at Indian Island. The head warden explained that one of the prisoners on the downed plane was awaiting the death penalty for murder and was considered extremely dangerous. He was Clyde Miller, the leader of the Miller gang that had been on the FBI's most wanted list. They were transferring him to another maximum-security prison because of his violent behavior. Sheriff Perkins ran over to Grandpa's house to relay the message before the search party left.

"Thanks for letting us know," said Grandpa. "We'll be extra careful, but I don't think we've got anything to worry about."

"Why's that?" asked the sheriff.

"Well, the odds of finding anyone alive up there are going to be slim and if someone does survive the crash, they're probably not going to be in any shape to cause much trouble. And don't forget, we have the Lord with us!" smiled Grandpa.

"Well, you be careful just the same," instructed Sheriff Perkins, I wouldn't want anything to happen to you or your grandkids." The sheriff gave Grandpa the radio antenna for tracking the emergency locator beacon and wished them all a safe trip.

Grandpa had decided to take the horses as far as they could. This would save them precious time getting to the back side of Bear Mountain.

"Boy, Grandpa, I'm sure glad we're riding the horses this time," said Taven.

"Me too," said Maddox, "It'll cut our travel time in half."

"That's why we need to take them," explained Grandpa. "Time will be very important to us in finding the crash site, especially if someone is still alive up in those mountains. We'll ride the horses as far as we can, then hobble them in the mountain meadow at the old prospector's cabin at the Caribou river till we get back. I've asked your friend, Rylee, if she would come along with us and watch the horses when we leave them at the base of the mountain. She got approval from her parents and will ride her own horse, that beautiful roan mare she calls 'Moon Beam'."

The kids were excited to have Rylee join them and continued to pack their supplies. Each kid had their own hand-picked horse they had raised from a colt. Aria had a palomino named Stardust, Taven had a black stallion named Tornado, and Maddox had a pinto named Thunder. The children loved to run their horses at full speed along the Caribou River trail in the evenings after school when their chores were done. When they raced with the wind in their faces with the sound of thundering hooves, they felt a sense of oneness with their swift and powerful friends. The smell of leather and horses and the creaking sound of the saddle were some of their fondest memories while living at Sawdust Springs.

After saddling the horses and loading their gear, the search and rescue party left the secure surroundings of Sawdust Springs. They headed for the back side of Bear Mountain, into the wild country that belonged to Single Claw. Grandpa, who was in charge of first aid, packed extra bandages and medicine in case they found any survivors at the crash site.

By evening, after traveling close to twelve miles, they had reached the end of the trail. From here on, they would have to make their way on foot. The steep, narrow trail that led through rocky landslides and steep drop offs were too dangerous for the horses to go. They hobbled the horses in a high mountain meadow filled with luscious grass and set up base camp for their return trip. Next to a river at the edge of the meadow was an old, abandoned miner's cabin. They had often stayed there when going on camp outs. It was the perfect shelter with a solid locked door, a wood stove and a watertight roof. Grandpa was glad Rylee had agreed to come along and watch the horses until they returned. She had always loved horses and knew it wouldn't be wise to leave them unattended. If one of them got tangled up in its hobble it could injure itself.

"Thanks, Rylee, for helping us," said Grandpa. "We shouldn't be gone more than two days. I'll leave you my shotgun in case any wolves or mountain lions decide to pay you a visit. It'll be very important that the horses are well taken care of for our return trip. Especially if we have any survivors with us that need to be carried out."

"You bet," said Rylee, I'll keep a close watch on them."

Grandpa reminded her that it was OK to have a fire in the stove since she was on the front side of Bear Mountain. Single Claw had never been seen on this side of the mountain.

"Don't worry about me," said Rylee, "I'll be O.K., especially with a safe warm cabin, a shotgun and Jesus by my side."

CHAPTER 2

AGAINST ALL ODDS

The next morning after a nice hot breakfast, they said their goodbyes to Rylee and headed further up the mountain. An eerie, thick fog was settling over the peaks, making visibility almost impossible.

Grandpa and the grandkids stopped to rest often because the trail leading into the mountains was steep and tiring especially with the heavy packs they were carrying. Knowing that somewhere in those rocky peaks was a downed plane with possible survivors gave them extra determination to keep up the pace. They stared up at the rugged landscape ahead and knew that finding the plane would be like looking for a needle in a haystack. They were glad they had the tracking beacon to follow, their chances of finding the crash site without it would be next to impossible.

Taven was wearing a set of earphones listening for the steady beep of the tracking beacon while Maddox carried the antenna alongside. Suddenly Taven stopped. He turned his head and then signaled for everyone to be quiet.

"I think I hear a faint signal. Yes, I've got a signal!" shouted Taven.

Everyone was anxious to know the direction it was coming from.

"Are you sure it's the emergency locator beacon," asked Aria?

" It's got to be," answered Taven. Maddox turned the antenna to find the strongest signal. The steady beep, beep, beep indicated it was coming from the northwest. "Let's go;" said Grandpa, "maybe we can find the crash site before nightfall."

He knew that the passengers' survival, if they were still alive, depended on how fast they were found and brought down from the mountain.

A half hour later when the trail rose above the treeline, the hikers had a clear view of Bear Mountain. The fog had lifted and off in the distance, high up on a narrow ledge, a small stream of smoke could be seen drifting upward in the evening sky.

"That must be them," said Aria. "Who else would be up in these mountains?"

"That's my thought, too," said Grandpa. "Let's try to get there before it's completely dark." They started hiking toward the smoke when Grandpa suddenly stopped with a worried look on his face.

"I wish right now we had packed your weapons but we didn't have room with all the first aid gear." he said.

"Why, Grandpa?" asked Taven.

"Remember where we are?" asked Grandpa. "We're on the back side of Bear Mountain. And what do you see up ahead?"

"I see a steep, rocky cliff and….." He stopped in mid sentence . "Smoke," said Taven. "I see smoke!" As he realized the danger that it meant. "I don't know how I could have forgotten. I guess the excitement of finding the crash sight clouded my thinking."

"Me too," said Maddox. "You don't suppose Single Claw has caught the scent of that fire, do you?"

"I don't know," answered Grandpa, "but we want to be ready if he has."

They all knew that Single Claw goes into a murderous rage every time he smells smoke. It reminds him of that horrible forest fire years ago that burned all the claws off his right paw, except one. That's why he's called Single Claw. Being much larger than a normal bear, he's the ruler of his mountain kingdom. No one knows for sure the number of people that have been his victim, but one thing is for sure, if you want to disappear on the backside of Bear Mountain, all you have to do is start a campfire.

The trail was rough going as it wound along the rocky cliffs. Grandpa decided to tie everybody together with a long rope just to be on the safe side. The danger of falling was of great concern as they climbed higher and higher.

As they got closer to the smoke, it became clear they had found where the plane had gone down. Broken pieces of the plane were scattered along the trail. Finally, when they rounded a bend, there it was, a scene of destruction that no one was prepared for.

"Jumping horney toads!" exclaimed Maddox. "I've never seen such wreckage in all my life."

"Me neither," said Aria. "There's nothing left of the plane."

The main body of the plane was ripped apart in three sections. One of the pieces rested precariously next to a thousand foot drop off. Half of it hung out into space and looked as if it would fall at any minute.

Grandpa gave instructions to scan the area for any survivors. "Stay away from the edge;" warned Grandpa. "I'll check the part of the plane that's hanging over the cliff."

Just then, Taven let out a shout. "Over here, come quick, someone's alive!" They all ran to where Taven was pointing. There, sitting by a small campfire, was a man huddled under a blanket.

"Is he still alive?" asked Aria.

Taven nodded, "I think so, I thought I saw him move."

Grandpa carefully pulled back the blanket to examine him. What he saw was a bloodied and broken man, stunned and in shock, but very much alive.

"It's a miracle!" said Grandpa. "Aria, get my first aid kit and check him out. I'll go look for the others!"

Before Grandpa crawled into the section of plane hanging dangerously over the cliff, he wrapped a rope around a rock and tied it to the plane. When he entered, he saw two men at the end of the wreckage that was hanging out over the edge. He knew he had to check for signs of life, but this would be extremely dangerous. His heart pounded when the plane shifted and rocked from his extra weight. He was glad he'd tied it off with the safety rope, especially when he looked down through a crack and saw the river a thousand feet below. He crawled cautiously toward the two men still strapped in their seat belts. When he reached them, he found no vital signs. They had died instantly from the crash. Backing out, he was relieved when his feet finally touched solid ground again.

"What did you find, Grandpa," asked Aria.

"There's two inside but they're both dead." Grandpa answered with a solemn voice. The words had no sooner left his mouth when the fuselage with the bodies in it shifted with a creaking noise. It teetered on the ledge and then slid off. The safety rope pulled down against a sharp rock and snapped into with a loud twang. The wreckage plunged down the thousand foot drop off making thunderous sounds that echoed back and forth off the cliffs. A cloud of dust encased the wreckage when it hit the bottom.

"Wow," gasped Grandpa. "I was just inside……I thought the safety rope would hold it. I guess it wasn't my time to die."

"I'm sure glad," said Maddox. "You've always said there's no need to worry about dying because God has all our days planned out and He has us in his hands."

"What about the bodies," asked Taven. "How will we get them back to Sawdust Springs?"

"We won't," answered Grandpa. "There's no way to get down that cliff. That will have to be their final resting place."

Just then Aria hollered, "Look! Over by that clump of brush. There's another body!" Everyone ran over to see if he was still alive.

After a close examination, Grandpa hollered, "Yes, he's alive, I can feel a pulse!" He was in a lot worse shape than the first one they found by the fire, but he was alive nonetheless. Unconscious from a blow on the head and possibly broken bones, Grandpa worked fast to stabilize his condition.

"Get some blankets out of my pack," ordered Grandpa, "We've got to get him warm and dry." They quickly covered him with warm blankets and carried him over to the campfire.

As they administered first aid to the two survivors, Aria asked, "Which ones are these? The pilot, the guard or the two prisoners?"

"Well," said Grandpa, "from the look of his tattered uniform and badge, this first one by the fire is the prison guard. Inside the plane, one was strapped in the pilots seat and the other one had striped clothes on. They had to be the pilot and one of the prisoners. This unconscious man is the other prisoner by the striped uniform he's wearing.

"Which prisoner do you think he is?" asked Aria. "Is he the dangerous one?"

"I don't know," answered Grandpa, "but we better assume he is just to be on the safe side. It's a good thing the prison guard managed to crawl out of the wreckage and start a fire, otherwise we might never have found them in time. Let's put out the fire before Single Claw gets a whiff of it."

Taven poured some water on the fire while Grandpa and Maddox began making an improvised stretcher with some sticks and a blanket.

"We'd better move out as quickly as we can," said Grandpa, "just in case Single Claw smelled the smoke. I think if I help hold the guard, he'll be able to walk." The guard didn't speak a word and seemed disoriented. He was still in shock from the crash.

"Grandpa," said Maddox, "We better get a move on. If Single Claw smells this fire, he'll be coming this way for sure."

Everyone agreed as they placed the unconscious prisoner on the stretcher.

Aria, being the oldest, took one end, Maddox and Tavin took the other.

Grandpa helped the guard to his feet with his arm around his shoulder and they all started down the mountain in haste, just in case Single Claw was coming.

They had traveled about an hour when Aria shouted, "he's waking up!" The injured prisoner laying on the stretcher began moving and mumbling incoherent words. They stopped and carefully set the stretcher down.

"Steady there mister, you're alright now," comforted Grandpa.

The man slowly opened his eyes and stared at his surroundings. "Where am I?" he muttered. "Where am I?"

"You're being taken to a hospital," said Grandpa, "You've just survived a terrible plane crash up on Bear Mountain."

The dazed man kept trying to talk. "The last thing," he paused and took a deep breath, "I remember, is…….. the plane having engine trouble."

"Just rest now, we can talk later. Right now, we need to keep moving."

When the injured man caught sight of the prison guard looking intently at him, a startled look came over his face. "Clyde, you're alive!" he whispered. But the guard acted like he didn't hear a thing. After staring for a few seconds, the prisoner laid his head back down on the stretcher and closed his eyes. Grandpa couldn't help but notice the confused look on his face.

Nearby in the rugged territory of Bear Mountain, Single Claw, the largest, meanest, most dangerous bear in the world was following the scent of smoke. Memories of the fire that had burned him years ago were stirring up his anger and rage as he got closer to the crash site.

The rescue party was only a mile down the trail when they heard a thunderous roar. Single Claw had come upon the wreckage! Growling and thrashing, he attacked the smoldering ashes, scattering them in all directions. Then, pieces of the plane were further ripped apart and thrown over the cliff as he vented his anger.

"Boy, I'm sure glad we got out of there when we did," exclaimed Maddox. They could hear terrible sounds of destruction coming from the crash site.

Grandpa ordered, "Keep moving before Single Claw catches our scent."

CHAPTER 3

TRAVELING WITH DANGER

A s our rescue party headed further down the mountain, they had no clue of the dangerous situation they were in.

"I'll sure be glad to get back to the horses," moaned an exhausted Maddox,

"Carrying this stretcher is hard work."

The injured man on the stretcher was heavy to carry and the guard, leaning on Grandpa's shoulder, hobbling in pain, slowed their progress considerably as they climbed down the steep mountain trail.

"It's starting to get dark," said Grandpa, "we better stop here for the night and get a fresh start in the morning."

Traveling on the rocky trail was hard enough in the daylight, but at night, the risk of falling would be too great. Besides, they were all in much need of rest and here was a good level spot for making camp.

After making a cozy shelter with fir boughs and blankets, Grandpa sat beside the guard, encouraging him that they would soon be back to civilization.

"How are you feeling now?" asked Grandpa. The guard had been very quiet and hadn't talked much as they came down the mountain.

"I'm doing better, just still shaken up. Having a hard time walking, that's all." He seemed irritated at Grandpa's question.

"Well, that's understandable," said Grandpa., "By the way, what's your name? Mine is Buck."

"Mine is Cly..., Ah....Clem Rogers, I'm the prison guard from Lone Pine."

Grandpa couldn't put his finger on it but something just didn't seem right.

He decided to wait till morning before asking any more questions.

"Well, you better try to get some rest now. We'll be back in Sawdust Springs sometime tomorrow," reassured Grandpa.

After a dinner of Indian flat bread and cold beans, Aria whispered to Grandpa,

"Did you notice something strange about the guard?"

"Like what?" asked Grandpa.

"Well, did you notice how his clothes don't fit very well? They're way too big for him."

"Yeah, now that you mention it, they don't fit too well. Maybe he just lost a lot of weight recently," reasoned Grandpa. Still, the suspicion Aria had only confirmed his own uneasiness.

"I'll see what I can find out in the morning," said Grandpa.

That night, they took turns keeping watch for Single Claw. He was close by and unpredictable. If he caught their scent, they knew he wouldn't hesitate to attack. Every sound in the darkness put their nerves on edge. It seemed like the night would never end. They were all glad when morning finally came, and the bright rays of sun dispelled the darkness.

"Rise and shine everybody," hollered Grandpa, "We need to have breakfast and get these men to a hospital. With any luck, I think we can reach the horses by late afternoon." Grandpa gave the guard the last granola bar and sat down beside him. Something wasn't right and he wanted to get to the bottom of it. After the usual small talk, the questions got more specific.

"How long have you been a law man?" asked Grandpa.

"Oh, about ten years," answered the guard.

"So you must know Sheriff Jones from Sawdust Springs," continued Grandpa.

"Yeah, sure, everybody knows Jones. He's been around a long time." The short slender man seemed nervous. He stared intently at Grandpa with cold steel eyes as he crunched up the granola bar wrapper.

"We're sure lucky to have a man like Jones for our sheriff." Grandpa was nervous and hoped it didn't show. He quickly excused himself and went over to where the grand kids were.

"Let's finish up as quick as we can and hit the trail." Secretly gesturing with his hand, he motioned them to follow him. When they got behind a small grove of trees, Grandpa whispered, "I think we've got trouble."

"Trouble?" repeated Aria. "What do you mean?"

"Well," continued Grandpa, "I asked the deputy if he knew Sheriff Jones from Sawdust Springs, and he said he did."

"Sheriff Jones!" said Taven, "Who's that? Everyone knows the sheriff at Sawdust Springs is Sheriff Perkins."

"That's right," said Grandpa, "and he has been for years. Every law man in the country knows Sheriff Perkins."

"Then why didn't the deputy know?" asked Maddox. "Is he just disoriented from the plane crash?"

"That's possible," answered Grandpa, "but maybe it's because our survivor isn't really the guard from the prison at all." answered Grandpa. "If my suspicions are right, we have an impostor on our hands who is pretending to be the prison guard."

"Then that's why his clothes don't fit," said Aria. "He must have changed clothes with the man we found in the bushes."

"He put on the guard's clothes and put his clothes on the guard making him look like one of the prisoners. And the person he exchanged clothes with is the one we have on the stretcher. See how tight his clothes fit." Explained Grandpa.

"That means our prison guard is really one of the prisoners and the one on the stretcher is really the prison guard." reasoned Aria. "Do you think he is the dangerous one?"

"I don't know," said Grandpa. "We must be careful not to let him know about our suspicions."

The sound of a gun being cocked made them all turn around. The impostor stepped out from behind the trees where he was overhearing their conversation and pointed his revolver straight at them.

"So, you figured it out did you? That's too bad. This will make things a little more complicated. One wrong move and it'll be your last."

CHAPTER 4

HELD HOSTAGE

B ack in the mountain meadow, Rylee had been waiting patiently for the return of the rescue party. Taking care of the horses had been easy. None of the horses had tangled up their hobbles and no mountain lions or wolves had come around looking for an easy meal. She was expecting the rescue party to be back last evening but gave up hope when they hadn't come by nightfall. They were a day overdue but that wouldn't be unusual, especially in the rough country around Bear Mountain. She checked the horses and then turned in for the night. The tent was cozy, and her sleeping bag was warm. Reading from her favorite book by flashlight was the best way to fall asleep. Each night the sound of howling wolves could be heard in the distance, but she wasn't afraid. Wolves don't usually attack when humans are around. At least that's what she'd been told. And besides, she had a shotgun if she needed it. Rylee was a very brave girl.

The rescue party backed slowly away from the man with the gun.

"All RIGHT, PUT YOUR HANDS IN THE AIR!" bellowed the impostor. They all raised their hands over their heads with eyes wide with fear. Grandpa realized that this man was Clyde Miller, the ringleader of the dangerous Miller Gang. On the FBI's ten most wanted list, Clyde Miller was awaiting the death penalty for the murder of more than fifteen people while leading his gang in a string of notorious bank robberies.

"My plan was foolproof until you, Mr. Grandpa, started snooping around and asking too many questions. Now keep your hands up and march."

Clyde gestured with his gun towards camp and limped close behind.

"Don't even think about escaping. Anyone trying to get away will be shot on the spot." They knew he meant what he said. The outlaw took some rope from Grandpa's pack and tied their hands behind their backs.

"And while we're tied up," asked Grandpa, "who's going to take care of your partner? He's the real prison guard, isn't he?"

"You mean that other jailbird?" smirked Clyde. He's nothing to me, just another lucky dope that survived the crash. I've got the same plans for him as I have for you. Can't afford to have any witnesses you know."

His lips curled in an evil grin followed by a sarcastic laugh.

Right then, they knew what his intentions were, and they weren't good.

"Grandpa," whispered Aria, "Is he planning on getting rid of us?"

"I'm afraid so," answered Grandpa, "but we're not going down without a fight."

The outlaw led them back to camp and made them sit on a log at the edge of the campsite. In front of them was Clyde Miller with a .38 Colt revolver he had taken off the real prison guard. He began taking the supplies he would need from their backpacks. Behind the log that they were sitting on was a fifteen foot drop off to the Caribou River.

Grandpa looked at the children and said, "We better pray."

Clyde laughed, "Yeah, you better pray alright. It's going to take a miracle to get you out of this one and I don't believe in miracles."

They closed their eyes and began praying quietly to themselves.

After a short while, Grandpa opened his eyes and talked in a quiet whisper. "I think the Lord has shown me a plan. It's not going to be easy, but it's the only hope we have."

"What is it?" whispered Maddox.

"Yeah," chimed in Taven, "how can we possibly get out of this one?" They huddled together, sitting on a log with Grandpa in the middle, Aria on his left and Taven and Maddox on his right.

"We must keep our voices down and not make any sudden moves," cautioned Grandpa. "He's keeping a close eye on us so look straight ahead while we're talking. Remember those two volunteers Sheriff Perkins sent out to look for Rawhide Jake last year." They all carefully signaled by nodding their head.

"Well, remember when Single Claw attacked them at their campsite, and they began running in the dark. What saved them?"

"They fell off the cliff into the river," whispered Aria.

"That's right. The way I see it we have the same situation with this drop off to the river right behind us." said Grandpa.

"But Grandpa, we don't have to get away from Single Claw, we have to escape from a killer outlaw," said Taven.

"I know," answered Grandpa, "That's where a little ingenuity comes in. Let's see if we can invite Single Claw to our farewell party."

"How will we do that?" asked Aria.

They all listened intently as Grandpa explained his plan.

"Are you sure that's going to work?" asked Taven, "It sounds pretty risky to me."

"It is risky," responded Grandpa, "But the odds of doing nothing are far worse. Is everyone in agreement?" They all nodded their heads. "OK then, we'll begin when I think the timing's right. Everyone must do their part exactly as I told you."

Aria started the plan by asking their abductor if he'd bring the injured prisoner on the stretcher closer to them. That way, she said, they could keep him calm if he became conscious.

"Why do you want to do that?" asked Clyde, "He's not going to be around much longer anyway. But having you all close together will make it easier for me to keep tabs on you." Clyde grabbed the corner of the stretcher and drugged him over to Aria.

The first part of the plan had worked. The wounded man now lay close to them when they would try to make their escape. He still remained unconscious.

"Now it's my turn," whispered Grandpa. "Hey Clyde, I've got a question for you."

"What is it?" snapped the outlaw.

"Well, everyone gets one last request before they die, don't they?"

"I suppose," said Clyde, "even those going to the electric chair in the big house get a last request. What is it you want?"

"Would it be too much trouble to have one last meal before we die?" asked Grandpa.

"No, I guess not." replied the killer. "I've got to eat too so we'll all join together for the 'last supper,' snickered Clyde, "Or should I say the last lunch."

"Would you fry us up some bacon and eggs? It's our favorite meal." asked Grandpa. "We've got plenty of food in our backpacks."

Clyde gathered some firewood and placed it directly in front of the tied up captives.

Taven's eyes bugged out.

"What's the matter with him," asked Clyde. "Hasn't he ever seen a campfire before?"

"Clyde, would you move the fire to the other side of the campsite, please?" pleaded Grandpa. "With the wind blowing in our faces and us not being able to move, it'll be pretty miserable with smoke in our eyes. You see, Taven is allergic to smoke."

"Yeah, I guess so." grumbled Clyde.

Grandpa and the grandkids breathed a sigh of relief. Everything was working as planned.

Finally, Clyde took out a match and lit the fire. He had no idea what he was getting himself into. The smoke drifted upward and filled the sky. It carried with it the only hope of escape for our rescue party. Finally, after about half an hour, their food was ready.

"Well, here you go," said Clyde as he dished up a slice of bacon and eggs into each tin plate. "I don't know why I'm doing this, but I hope you enjoy your last meal."

The outlaw untied their hands then dished up a large plate for himself and sat over by the fire with his gun pointed in their direction.

Grandpa instructed the kids to eat slowly and buy as much time as they could. While they were eating, Clyde checked the pistol, making sure it was fully loaded. He only needed five bullets to carry out his evil plan. He began to pace back and forth in front of them, fidgeting with his gun as the tension mounted. Finally, he spun around and hollered, "Hurry up and finish! It's time to get this over with."

"Grandpa," said Maddox, "Our plan didn't work." Clyde overheard something about a "plan."

"Plan! What plan?" he hollered. "You weren't planning to escape, were you?" he sneered. "Well, I guess your little plan didn't work. There's no way you can get away from me now." He turned to Grandpa and heckled, "OK old man, stand up and be the first to go. Show us how to die like a man."

Grandpa stood to his feet and turned for one final look at his grandkids.

"We tried," he said., "That's all we could do." Everyone was teary-eyed.

Clyde leveled the revolver at Grandpa and was starting to squeeze the trigger when a twig snapped from behind him. He glanced back and froze with fear at what he saw. Standing at the edge of the clearing was a dark, towering figure. A fifteen-foot-tall monster snarling and clawing the air. Single Claw! With a roar that shook the ground, the grizzly started towards him. Clyde began firing his pistol at the gigantic bear, only to see the bullets bounce off his thick hide.

"Now!" said Grandpa. Aria, Taven and Maddox picked up the stretcher with the injured man and jumped off the cliff to the river below. The fall was the scariest thing they had ever experienced. The wind rushed in their faces as they fell to what might be an icy grave. Holding on to the stretcher, they plunged into the cold water and sank out of site. After several seconds, they rose to the surface, gasping for air, holding the injured man above the water. The exhilaration was beyond description as they began drifting down the river, alive and well. It was a miracle that all had survived the fall without injury. Looking around in the water, Aria cried out, "Where's Grandpa?" Frantically, they all searched but Grandpa wasn't anywhere to be found.

Taven dove beneath the water looking for him but found nothing.

Up at the campsite they could hear the roar of Single Claw as he tore up the campsite. The bear turned and slowly began walking toward Clyde, swaying his head back and forth with saliva dripping from his mouth. The frightened man couldn't move fast because of his injuries. He knew this was the end of the line. Single Claw reared up on his hind legs and raised his paw for one final, deadly sweep. Clyde closed his eyes.

Just when he thought it was all over, something grabbed the back of his coat and jerked him to the ground. He found himself being dragged to the edge of the cliff with the giant bear walking towards him. With a superhuman effort, Grandpa flung Clyde and himself over the edge. Single Claw missed them by inches with the swish of his paw.

Coming up out of the water, Clyde was choking and coughing with Grandpa keeping his head above the surface.

"There's Grandpa!" hollered Maddox. "And he's got that killer with him!"

They swam over to them and grabbed hold of their arms, helping each other keep afloat as they drifted downstream away from that killer bear.

The rescue party drifted until they were far away from danger before coming to shore and drying off.

"Wow, Grandpa," said Aria, "your plan worked. Single Claw saved our lives."

"The Lord saved us, children," answered Grandpa, "Sometimes He even uses our enemies to deliver us."

"But Grandpa," asked Maddox, "Why did you risk your life saving that awful man? After all, he was going to kill us."

"Believe me," said Grandpa, "I did wrestle with the thought of it. I just felt compelled to do what Jesus would want me to do."

"What's that?" interrupted Taven.

"To do good and show God's love to everyone, even to our enemies. Clyde will get his justice when we turn him over to the authorities, he's not escaping that. The important thing is to have a clear conscience in this whole matter. Besides, he won't give us any more trouble without that gun. He's so busted up he can hardly walk."

Clyde sat shivering from the cold, looked up at Grandpa and said,

"Man, I don't understand you. I was going to shoot you and you saved my life."

It was the first time in his life he had experienced anything like that.

After drying off, Grandpa explained to Clyde that starting a fire on the back side of Bear Mountain is the surest way to attract that bear. "I knew that you didn't know this because of the fire you'd started back at the crash site. I'm just glad it all worked out the way it did. I'm going to tie your hands together just to be on the safe side. I think you understand why."

Clyde nodded his head and did as he was told.

It was early afternoon when they finally came down from the mountain and reached the cabin where Rylee and the horses were. Were they ever glad to see each other. They raced across the meadow with tears of joy streaming down their faces. The hugs flowed freely. Even the horses got a few.

"Wow, am I glad to see you guys!"said Rylee. "I was worried sick that something bad had happened to you."

"And we're glad to see you," said Aria. "We didn't think we'd ever see you again. Wait till you hear what happened to us up at the crash site."

Rylee noticed they had two survivors with them. One of them had his hands tied and the other was on a stretcher. After warming up by the wood stove in the cabin, they explained to her everything that had happened.

"Wow," she exclaimed. "And I thought I had its rough staying here by myself listening to the wolves at night. I kept thinking, that if I was with you, it would be a lot safer."

They all broke out in uncontrollable laughter.

After loading up the horses they started the final leg of their journey back to Sawdust Springs. Clyde riding double with Grandpa and the real prison guard being towed Indian style on a stretcher, called a travois, behind one of the horses. Late that evening they arrived at Sawdust Springs and turned Clyde over to Sheriff Perkins at the city jail. They told him everything that happened and explained how Single Claw was used by God to save their lives. The Sheriff shook his head in amazement and said, "What a story. I'm just glad to see everyone is still alive after what you went through!"

"So are we!" they all said in unison.

"Enough talking," interrupted Grandpa. "We need to get this injured man over to Doc Barns so he can get some medical attention."

The next day the local newspaper caught wind of this incredible story and it wasn't long before everyone in the far north heard about it. The title was: 'The Bear hunters did it again!" How they rescued two survivors from a Bear Mountain Plane Crash.

Grandpa and the grandkids visited Clyde several times in prison. He wanted to learn more about a God that could love him, like was demonstrated to him back up on the mountain. His sentence for a life of crime was finally served but not before making peace with God. The injured prison guard had a complete recovery after several months of rehab at the hospital at Pleasantville.

A powerful lesson was learned by all.

STORY FOUR

ESCAPE FROM BEAR MOUNTAIN

CHAPTER 1

SETTING THE TRAP

As the car turned into the dark, backstreet alley, Bill Morgan couldn't stop thinking that this was the strangest story he'd ever written. For the past twelve years as senior editor of a popular outdoor magazine called Wilderness Fishing, he'd written many a story about the sport but none like this. All his other stories were true, but this one was totally false from the beginning. He had written it for money. The thought of making a quarter of a million dollars for just one story was just too much to turn down. He hadn't been told and he hadn't asked why the caller wanted an article about trophy-sized trout caught in an unknown river of the far north. Anyway, all the fish stories get stretched a little, he thought, trying to sooth his conscience. As he drove down the dark alley, he was glad tonight would be the final payoff.

Suddenly, a man stepped out in front of the car! Skidding to a halt, Bill rolled down the window and hollered, "Hey, mister, you better be more careful! I almost ran you over!"

"And how are you tonight, Mr. Morgan?" the stranger answered back in a calm voice.

Surprised that the man knew his name, Bill realized this must be the mysterious person who had requested the phony article. Tonight's payoff was their first meeting, face to face.

"Uh, I'm fine Mr...?

"Never mind who I am," snapped the stranger. "I just need to ask you a couple questions before you get your final payment. First, will the article be coming out in this month's issue?"

"Yeah, just like I promised," answered Bill.

"And then," continued the stranger, "did you tell anyone about our little business venture?"

"No, not a soul, that was part of the agreement."

The stranger smiled as he reached into his briefcase and pulled out a large sack full of money. "You did real good Bill; now don't forget, no one will ever know anything about this."

"Sure thing, for the amount of money you've paid me, I won't even tell the Lord on Judgment Day about our little secret. I'll do whatever you tell me." As the stranger turned and walked away, Bill noticed the initials, 'J. H.' in the corner of the stranger's briefcase. That was all he knew about the mysterious man who wanted a fictitious fishing article printed in his magazine.

<hr>

The five o'clock whistle had just blown at the Olson Tractor and Implement Company. Emery and Jack were third generation owners of the prosperous business. Emery was the oldest brother and senior partner, something Jack had always resented. His hopes of being more than a junior partner looked pretty slim since Emery had a son who would someday inherit his dad's position.

But today Jack walked into Emery's office at closing time in unusually high spirits. He was whistling.

"Well, big brother," smiled Jack, "how has your week gone?" Jack knew that Emery was still recovering from his wife's death of cancer last year and could use some cheering up. Before Emery could answer, Jack pulled out a magazine from his briefcase.

"What have you got there?" asked Emery. "Something has sure got you wound up."

"Well, I've been thinking. Ever since Marge died, you haven't taken one day off. Josh will be ten years old next week and I'll bet you haven't even thought about doing something with him, have you?"

"Well, no, not really," answered Emery.

"Just what I thought," nodded Jack. "Now take a look at this."

Jack opened the current issue of *Wilderness Fishing* and turned to the article about giant rainbow trout. "Have you ever seen trout this size before?"

"Wow," said Emery, "look at the size of those monsters!"

"Well, here's what I've done," continued Jack. "I know how Josh loves to fly fish, so I went ahead and bought him his birthday present."

"And what might that be?" asked Emery, one eyebrow raised.

"It's a three-day fishing trip to where those trophy fish were caught. I've reserved a bush plane to fly you and Josh there next week."

Emery was speechless. Never had his younger brother done anything like this before.

"I don't know what to say," said Emery.

"Just say you'll accept," urged Jack, "You need some time away from this place."

"I guess you're right," said Emery., "I have been pretty focused on my work since Marge...," he paused with a lump in his throat, then continued.

"Just where is this place, anyway?"

Jack knew then he'd convinced his older brother. "According to this article, it's a place of peace and solitude in the far north. You'll be going to the Caribou River. It's somewhere on the backside of a place called....... Bear Mountain. If you're going to go, you'll have to hurry. Freeze up is coming to that northern area in about three weeks."

Four days later a bush pilot was landing his plane on a remote gravel bar on the Caribou River, unloading his two passengers and their gear.

The cold night air signaled the fast approach of winter to the far north. Freeze-up was just a few weeks away. All the rivers and lakes would soon be frozen solid. Winter temperatures of forty below zero weren't uncommon at Sawdust Springs. That's why a warm cabin like Grandma and Grandpa's was so appreciated by their three grandkids, Aria, Taven and Maddox, who sat by the warm glow of the fireplace sipping hot chocolate and playing board games. This was their first full year in Sawdust Springs. Their parents purchased the general store, and it was proving to be a good decision. Now the family could be together throughout the whole year, not just a few weeks in the summer. The evenings spent at Grandma and Grandpa's cabin were special times of family bonding that the children would never forget.

The tranquil scene was interrupted when the phone rang.

"I'll get it," said Grandpa. "Hello...why yes, Sheriff Perkins, how can I help you?... Are you serious? When did this happen?... Well, I don't know, I'll have to talk it over with them... OK, I'll let you know in the morning."

"What did Sheriff Perkins want?" asked Aria. "Is someone in trouble?"

"It sure sounds like it," said Grandpa. "A father and son are overdue from a fishing trip. Sheriff Perkins wants to know if we can go looking for them."

"You bet we can," said Maddox. "Do you know what lake they were fishing at?"

"Well, that's the problem," answered Grandpa. "They weren't fishing in a lake but a river, the Caribou River. The headwaters of the Caribou, to be precise."

Taven's eyes widened. "You mean they went to the backside of Bear Mountain to go fishing?"

"I'm afraid so," answered Grandpa. "Evidently they're not from around here or they'd have heard of the trouble we've been having up there with Single Claw."

"Who are they anyway?" asked Aria, "Did Sheriff Perkins know anything about them?"

"He said he had some important information he wanted to go over with us in the morning; that is, if we decide to go," said Grandpa.

Grandpa wanted unanimous agreement before he talked to Sheriff Perkins. "Is everyone ready for another search and rescue trip to Bear Mountain?"

"Yes!" they all answered in unison.

"We've been training hard with our weapons and we're anxious to go," answered Aria.

"All right," said Grandpa, "I'll tell Sheriff Perkins we'll head out tomorrow, right after we meet with him to go over the search plans."

Excitement was in the air as they packed for another adventure. This time, with their weapons, they would be prepared if Single Claw gave them any trouble.

CHAPTER 2

THE SEARCH BEGINS

It was still dark outside when they all sat down to a breakfast of hot pancakes, bacon and eggs. Anticipation was in the air as they hurriedly finished their meal and bundled up for their walk to Sheriff Perkins office. The silence of the early dawn was broken only by the sound of footsteps crunching through the frozen snow. All over Sawdust Springs you could see straight streams of smoke rising from chimneys into the still, chilly dawn. The tingling cold made their breaths look like little steam engines. It felt good to open the door to the sheriff's office and feel the warm blast of heat from a pot-bellied wood stove.

"Come on in," said the Sheriff, "Warm yourselves up by the stove while I get you some hot chocolate." Grandpa and the Bear Hunters took off their heavy coats and huddled around the warm stove. In a few minutes, the Sheriff came back carrying a tray full of steaming mugs. "Buck," the sheriff said, "first I want to thank you and your grandkids for volunteering. I can always count on you when I need help. But there is more to this story that you need to know." They all listened intently as the sheriff began. "You've heard of the Olson tractor company, haven't you?"

"Sure," said Grandpa, "I think everybody's heard of it. They build the best farm equipment in the country. What does that have to do with our lost fisherman?"

"Well, our lost fisherman happens to be Emery Olson, the great grandson of John Olson who started the company years ago. Emery Olson is one of the wealthiest men in the world.!"

"Jumping horny toads!" exclaimed Maddox, "What's a rich man like that doing in our part of the country?"

"Good question," said the sheriff. "I'd like to know the answer to that as well. I got a call from his younger brother saying he was worried about Emery and his boy when they missed the bush plane that was supposed to pick them up yesterday. The pilot said he waited for them till dark before taking off. He drew me a map showing where they were supposed to meet. It's a gravel bar on the Caribou River about ten miles north of Bear Mountain."

"This map doesn't give us much to go on," said Aria. "This isn't going to be easy."

"I know," answered the sheriff. "My suggestion would be to head out as soon as you can because freeze-up could come any day now and make it impossible to follow any footprints. If things go well, you should be able to reach the headwaters of the Caribou River in a couple of days."

"We'll be able to leave by 10:00 o'clock since we're almost packed," said Grandpa.

They hurried home and finished gathering their supplies. After saying their good -by's to Grandma and their parents, they headed north into the rugged territory of

Bear Mountain. The first day they made it as far as the Ranger Station at Loon Lake, their normal stopping place. After supper, Grandpa got out the map and showed the kids the search area.

"I sure hope they're OK," said Taven.

"Me too," agreed Grandpa. "We've got to find them before Single Claw does. If he hasn't already."

The next day began with the steep climb up from Loon Lake. A light snow was on the ground with a constant threat of more. After a couple of miles, they came to the spot where the hidden trail forks off towards the secret caves of Bear Mountain. No one knows this place except Grandpa, the Grand kids, and Rawhide Jake. They make sure a brush pile keeps it concealed. "Hey," said Aria, "Remember last year when we took a break right here and found the hidden trail? Are we going that way again?" "No," said Grandpa, "we need to stay on the main trail. It leads further north to the headwaters of the Caribou River. But from here on out, remember, no more campfires. We don't want any uninvited guests like Single Claw."

When they reached the river, they followed the gravel bars whenever they could. After about a mile, Maddox noticed some tracks on the river's edge. "Look everybody, footprints!" After examining them closely, they concluded they were from an adult and a child.

"Looks like we're on the right trail," encouraged Grandpa. "This has to be the tracks of Emery Olson and his son Josh. Keep a close watch for more tracks."

At the end of the day, they hadn't found any more signs of the overdue fishermen. The sun was setting on the Caribou River, and it was time to set up camp.

Off in the distance, a lone wolf howled as the full moon began to rise over Bear Mountain, a sound they never tired of hearing. "I love to hear the howl of wolves," said Taven.

"Me too," said Aria. "It's like dinner music in the far north."

"I'm just glad we have our weapons," chimed in Maddox, "just in case those wolves might like us for dinner."

"Yeah," agreed Grace., "I know wolves aren't supposed to attack people, but it doesn't hurt to be prepared." Without a campfire their meals consisted of beef jerky and Indian soup. Flour mixed with water to a consistency of thick mud. It wasn't very tasty but was very nutritious. They also took vitamins to supplement their diet. Staying warm and dry wasn't a problem since they had the best insulated clothing in the world, goose down and gore-tex.

Sleep came easy as our tired search party crawled into their warm sleeping bags.

The next morning, a light sprinkling of snow covered the ground. It brought renewed hope of finding the lost fishermen since their tracks would be much easier to locate. What they didn't need was more snow that would cover the fresh tracks over again.

As they started hiking up the trail, Aria was curious. "Why would that man bring his son way up here to go fishing? Doesn't he know the danger of Single Claw?"

Not to mention the wolves and mountain lions and the harsh winter coming on.

"Good question," answered Grandpa., "He probably thought the trophy trout in these waters was worth the risk. Since no one ever fishes in this area, the trout grow to record size."

While they were discussing the foolish choice of risking your life for a few fish, Aria made a startling discovery. "Over here, I've found more tracks!"

She had found more footprints all right, but this time there was another set right behind the fishermen, and they were bear tracks. And it wasn't just any bear; the lone claw mark on the right paw indicated it belonged to only one bear, Single Claw!

"This doesn't look good," said Grandpa. "Single Claw is following them. We've got to catch up to them before that killer bear does!"

CHAPTER 3

CAMPFIRE OF DANGER

That evening, a father and son sat beside a warm, glowing fire enjoying the best dinner on earth. Fresh caught trout, skillet-fried in butter over an open campfire, seasoned with fresh air, exercise and a huge appetite.

"Boy dad, I'm sure glad uncle Jack thought of this fishing trip. I'm having the best birthday of my life."

"I'm glad we came too," added Emery. "I needed to get away and spend some time with you. And Josh was right about these fish, they're the biggest trout I've ever seen."

"Dad, after dinner, can we walk down to the river and fish a little more before it gets completely dark?" Josh just couldn't get enough fishing in. He loved it so much.

"I suppose, but just a little while," answered his dad. "I'm just about ready to hit the hay."

Grabbing their poles they headed off down the trail toward the river. Each cast brought a strike. Using barbless hooks made it easy to release the fish they didn't want to keep without injuring it.

They were just about ready to head back to camp when they heard it, a roar that was so loud it shook the trees. Then came a commotion from their campsite that sounded like an explosion.

"What is it, Dad? I'm scared!"

"Be really quiet, son. It sounds like a huge bear!"

The Growling and snapping of teeth kept up for about fifteen minutes. Small trees snapped like matchsticks and everything they owned was shredded to pieces....... and then all was quiet. Single Claw was sniffing the air, trying to locate the inhabitants of the campsite. Emery was glad they were down by the river. He knew they would have probably died if they had remained in their camp that evening.

No one had warned them about Single Claw, the largest, meanest bear in the world. Years ago, a forest fire had burned all the claws off on his right paw, except one. When he smells smoke, it brings back memories of the terrible fire that burned him so bad and he goes into a murderous rage. Anyone familiar with the area knows never to start a campfire on the back side of Bear Mountain.

Emery and his son Josh waited to see if the creature that attacked their campsite had left. A few minutes went by, and all remained quiet. Then they heard some branches snap. Something was coming down the trail to the river, right towards them!

"Quick," whispered Emery, "follow me." Throwing down their fishing rods, Emery and Josh took off along the river's edge as fast as they could. They stumbled over rocks and fallen trees in the twilight.

"Over here, Dad!" panted Josh. "There's a trail going off into the brush!" Quickly, they darted up an old deer trail that led away from the river. Behind them, they could hear brush snapping and growls from an angry bear. They knew the monster was still after them. Fortunately, they were downwind from the bear, making it difficult for the animal to smell their scent.

"Roooar." The loud roar sent shivers down their spines. Then it was quiet as the bear stopped dead in his tracks, listening for any sign of his escaping victims.

"Quiet," said Emery, "He's stopped chasing us. I think he's listening for us." They waited until they could hear the bear moving through the brush again, and then took off running as fast as they could. They played this cat and mouse game several times before reaching the base of the mountain.

In front of them was a steep wall of rock that towered high above the trail. Then Josh heard a thud behind him. He turned around and saw his Dad on the ground holding his ankle. He rushed back.

"What happened Dad? Are you alright?"

Emery shook his head, no. "I tripped on a rock and twisted my ankle pretty bad. I don't know if I can go any further."

"You have to!" cried Josh., "That creature will be on us any minute!"

Emery tried to walk but fell back down. He lay on the ground, looking up at the rock cliffs just above them. Then he saw it. "Look, up there! It's a cave!"

Josh looked up and saw the small cave on the side of the mountain. Sticking out of the cave's entrance was an old, fallen tree.

"Dad!" shouted Josh, "We've got to climb up to that cave!" Without hesitating, Josh reached into his backpack and pulled out a rope. "If I can lasso that snag up there, we can pull ourselves up!" It's our only chance of escape!

On the third try, Josh managed to lasso his rope around a limb on the old tree. "Hurry!" said his dad, "Get up there!" Josh grabbed the rope and, in a flash, pulled himself up to the safety of the cave.

"Now dad!" yelled Josh. "It's your turn!"

"I don't know if I can," responded Emery. "My leg's in pretty bad shape."

"You must!" pleaded Josh. "Hurry!"

Emery took hold of the rope and tried to pull himself up. "I can't," said Emery., "My leg is like an anchor. It won't hold my weight and I can't climb the rope."

Just then, there was a loud growl coming out of the dark woods.

"Hurry Dad!" screamed Josh. He knew every minute counted to save his dad's life.

"I've got an idea," yelled Emery. He tied a loop in the bottom of the rope and put his good foot in it. "When I step up, pull on the rope!"

Josh pulled with all his might. "It's working Dad," he shouted as his dad slowly inched his way up the steep rock wall. He was almost to the cave when the largest bear in the world stepped into the clearing. When the giant beast saw the man struggling up the rope, he stood on his hind legs and gave another thunderous roar. Then he charged, jumping high in the air and slashing at the helpless man.

With his last ounce of strength, Emery pulled himself up and over the ledge of the cave, just in time. He could feel the air from the powerful paw, swishing by him.

"Wow, that was close, Dad!" shouted Josh.

"Too close," gasped Emery.

They watched the bear pace back and forth, trying to figure out a way to get to them. All that night, they could hear the bear down below, pacing, snarling, scratching at the rocks. But at least for now, they were safe in their high, mountain cave. Fortunately, they had a few supplies and matches that Josh had in his backpack.

CHAPTER 4

SEARCHING FOR MORE CLUES

G randpa, Aria, Taven and Maddox followed the tracks of the lost fishermen as fast as they could. "I sure hope we're not too late," said Grandpa, "From the looks of these tracks, Single Claw is still following them. It won't be long before that bear catches up to them."

A couple more miles of following tracks brought our rescue team to an all too familiar sight, a campsite that had been completely torn to pieces.

"Oh no!" said Aria, "we're too late!"

"It sure looks like it," agreed Taven.

"Hold on now," interrupted Grandpa. "Before we jump to any conclusions, let's see if there are any remains of the fishermen in all this rubble."

They began the unpleasant, gruesome task of looking for what might be the remains of two bodies. Relief came over everyone when they didn't find anything.

"Jumping hornytoads!" exclaimed Maddox. "Somehow they must have gotten away!"

Aria was still searching the area when she noticed tracks leading down to the river. "Look over here everyone! This is where they escaped!"

Following the tracks, they found two fishing rods lying on the muddy riverbank.

"They must have been down here fishing when Single Claw attacked their camp," said Grandpa. "Look around for any more clues."

It wasn't long before they were following three sets of tracks again, two human and one bear. From the distance between the tracks, they could tell that the father and son were running, running for their lives from the most dangerous bear in the world, Single Claw!

———————)❦(———————

Back at the Olson Tractor Company, Jack Olson sat in his brother's office. He was leaning back in his brother's chair with his feet on the desk, looking at the article about giant trout in the Caribou River that he'd paid to have written in the *Wilderness Fishing* magazine.

"Soon this business will all be mine," he thought. He had learned about Bear Mountain from a newspaper article last year. A plane had crashed there, and a giant bear called Single Claw had tried to kill the rescue team (Grandpa and the Bear Hunters). A smile crept over his face at the thought of that bear making him sole owner of the business. But then the smile faded. "It wasn't fair," he argued to himself, "Pa should have made me the senior partner." Envy, greed and pride had been Jack's downfall ever since he had rejected the moral teachings of his parents when he was a teenager. "But now I'll finally have what's due me," he thought.

Little did he know how true that would be.

———)❈(——

Back at Sawdust Springs, Sheriff Perkins, with coffee cup in hand, stepped out onto his front porch. He couldn't believe what he saw. Coming into town was a caravan of television news trucks. FOX News, CNN, ABC and NBC were pulling up in front of the Sheriff's office. Before he had time to think, reporters were swarming around him like bees on honey.

"Are you Sheriff Perkins?"

"Have you started a search for Emery Olson?"

"Give us an update on the situation!" Questions were coming quicker than he could answer.

"Now hold on a minute! One at a time, please," hollered the Sheriff. "Give me time to answer."

"Yes, I'm Sheriff Perkins and I've got my best people looking for the two lost fishermen. Buck and his grandkids."

"And who are they?" asked one of the reporters.

The sheriff paused for a moment. They are called the Bear Hunters. Composed of a grandfather and his three Grandkids. They have been the most successful at rescuing people lost up in Bear Mountain.

"What!" exclaimed one of the reporters., "You've got a grandfather and his grandchildren looking for one of the wealthiest men in the country?"

"That's right," responded the sheriff., "They are the only ones I trust up there on Bear Mountain to survive against Single Claw."

"Single Claw!" shouted a reporter, "Who's Single Claw?"

Sheriff Perkins explained about the giant bear that lives on the back side of Bear Mountain and how the Bear Hunters were the only ones experienced enough to go on a search and rescue party in that part of the mountain.

"So far," he said, "We hadn't heard back from them, but if anyone could find Emery and his son Josh, they could."

"Man, this is going to be one hot story," whispered one of the reporters to another, "Just imagine, one of the richest men in the country being rescued by a grandfather and his grandkids. Our readers will eat it up!"

"Maybe," answered his friend, "If that bear doesn't eat them up first. It'll be a miracle if they come back alive."

One of the reporters held up a magazine. "Sheriff, this article about large, trophy-sized trout in the Caribou River doesn't mention anything about a bear called Single Claw."

"What article?" asked Sheriff Perkins, "Let me see that magazine. I'd like to read it."

The reporter stepped forward and handed the rolled-up magazine to the sheriff.

The press meeting ended a few minutes later with a stern warning from the sheriff that no one was to go looking for Emery and his son. The danger was just too great, he said, and he didn't have the manpower for another search and rescue.

That evening Sheriff Perkins read the article in the *Wilderness Fishing* magazine. He couldn't believe what he read. "Who in their right mind would write some-thing like this without any warning about Single Claw?" he mumbled out loud. "And why?" He wondered how many more fishermen might be on their way to the Caribou River looking for trophy-sized trout after reading that story.

CHAPTER 5

DISCOVERY IN THE CLIFFS

Grandpa and the Bear Hunters were following the trail of the lost fishermen. They were hurrying over some large boulders when Grandpa lost his balance and started to fall. He caught himself, avoiding injury, but his old 30/30 rifle slipped out of his hand and crashed on some rocks below.

"Hold up everyone, I've dropped my rifle!"

The Bear Hunters watched Grandpa climb down to retrieve his gun and saw a disappointed look on his face as he picked up his rifle in two broken pieces. "It looks like I've done it now," said a disgusted Grandpa. "The lever action is broken."

"Now what will we do?" said Maddox. "We don't have a gun!"

"That's right," said Grandpa, "but you still have your weapons. If we turn back now, those two fishermen won't have a chance." After talking it over, they decided to continue. They hadn't gone far when Taven noticed something off in the distance. "Look! Up there on the side of the mountain. It looks like smoke coming from a cave!"

Sure enough, as they got closer, they could see smoke drifting from the entrance of a small cave.

"That must be the lost fishermen," said Aria. "They don't know how much Single Claw hates fires."

"Get your weapons ready!" instructed Grandpa. "We're in Single Claw's territory now. Anytime there's smoke, he's bound to be close by!"

They quietly made their way to the clearing beneath the cave. After finding no sign of the killer bear, Grandpa hollered, "Hello! Is anybody there?" They were staring up at the cave where the smoke was coming from when suddenly a man and a boy appeared at the entrance. They both began yelling and waving their hands with joy and disbelief that they had finally been found.

"Hurry! Get up here!" yelled Emery, "There's the biggest bear I've ever seen down there trying to get us. He leaves for a while then comes back. He's never gone long."

The father and son lowered the rope for the rescue party to climb up. Aria climbed up first and then Taven. Maddox was just starting up the rope when a growl was heard in the woods.

"Quick, get up there!" yelled Grandpa. Maddox rolled into the cave as Grandpa started his climb up the rope.

"Single Claw's coming!" They yelled! Grandpa was halfway up the rope when the bear came into sight. He reared on his hind legs and gave a thunderous roar. Grandpa set a world record on rope climbing that day. He scrambled up the rope like an Olympic athlete and threw himself into the cave's entrance as Single Claw exploded out of the woods.

"Boy, that was close!" said Aria.

"It sure was," panted Grandpa. "It's amazing what a little adrenaline can do."

"Yeah," said Taven, "This cave is a real lifesaver."

After the Bear Hunters calmed down from their climb and close call, Grandpa introduced themselves. He explained that the bear was Single Claw and told the story about his hatred of fires.

"So that's it," said Emery. "That explains why he attacked our campsite and why he keeps coming back to this cave." Emery told how they escaped along the river and literally stumbled onto this cave.

"It's a miracle," said Grandpa. "You're fortunate to be alive. Most people coming into this territory don't live to tell about it! What brought you way out here to Bear Mountain, in the first place?"

Emery said they had seen a magazine article about giant trout in the Caribou River. His brother, Jack, had paid for the whole trip as a birthday present for Josh.

"Didn't the magazine article mention anything about Single Claw?" asked Grandpa.

"Not a word," answered Emery. "If it had, there's no way we would have come."

"I'd sure like to know who wrote that story," said Grandpa. "No one ever fishes this part of the Caribou River. The fish are big alright, but it's much too dangerous because of that killer bear. It's downright criminal to write an article like that without warning about Single Claw."

"I'm sure my brother, Jack, didn't have a clue about that bear, or he never would have sent us up here," said

Emery. "What I'm concerned about now is, how are we going to get back?"

"That's where we come in," said Grandpa. "With the Lord's help, we'll get you and your son back home safe and sound."

While Grandpa and Emery talked, the kids sat down beside the fire and got better acquainted.

"Hi Josh, I'm Maddox, how old are you?"

"I just turned ten," answered Josh. "Dad brought me up here to celebrate my tenth birthday. We were having the time of our lives until we met that bear you call Single Claw. Boy, are we ever glad to see you guys."

Aria and Taven also introduced themselves and told Josh about their mission; to help those in need and rescue people from Single Claw.

"Yeah," said Maddox, "we're known around these parts as the Bear Hunters. We never kill any bears, only rescue others from Single Claw. Sheriff Perkins uses us as deputies whenever he needs help."

Josh was impressed that kids could do such an important job. "I noticed the weapons you have. Where did you get all that neat equipment?"

"We had them specially made," answered Aria, "They're the best money can buy."

Aria held up her titanium bow and graphite arrows. Taven showed his shield and helmet made from carbon fiber and his sword made of 440 stainless steel. Then Maddox proudly displayed his balanced throwing knives with industrial diamond edges and his spear made of Kevlar handles with a tungsten steel blade.

"And I'm the paramedic," said Grandpa. I carry a medical kit for helping anyone that might get injured. I also usually carry a rifle, but I just broke it when it fell on some rocks."

"Wow!" said Josh, "I've never seen anyone like you guys! You must be the bravest people in the world!"

"Well," responded Aria, "we practice a lot, but our real help comes from God. He's the only reason we can stand up against a bear like Single Claw."

They could have talked all night, but Grandpa thought it best to turn in and get some sleep. He stoked the fire so they could endure the extreme cold. Freeze up was just arriving and the temperature was rapidly dropping. The Caribou River would soon be frozen solid.

"I'm sure glad we can have a fire up in this cave," said Maddox, "I think we would freeze without it. Besides, Single Claw can never get us up here."

That night as Emery tried to go to sleep, he had one question on his mind – how were they going to escape from that giant bear called Single Claw? They were safe for the moment but were also prisoners without a way out.

CHAPTER 6

PLANS FOR ESCAPE

The next morning, Grandpa was the first to crawl out of his sleeping bag. The sun was just a faint glow on the frozen landscape. The temperature had reached thirty below that night. He peered down from the cave and saw Single Claw pacing back and forth, making sure his captives didn't get away.

"Doesn't that bear ever hibernate?" asked Emery as he walked up beside Grandpa with his sleeping bag wrapped around him. "I thought they were supposed to sleep in a den all winter."

"Most bears do, but I'm not sure about this one. There's been reports of trappers disappearing in the middle of winter up in this area. We used to think it was the harsh winter conditions that got them, but now I'm not so sure, seeing that Single Claw isn't in hibernation. That bear will want to store up fat for the long, cold winter. And right now, he wants us for his food supply. How often does Single Claw leave the cave and how long does he stay away before returning?" asked Grandpa.

"Two or three times a day for about an hour each time." answered Emery.

"That's what I was hoping," said Grandpa, "We'll have to watch when he leaves so we can go down and work on our escape plan."

"And just what is your plan?" asked Emery.

"Have you ever ridden on an ice sled?" questioned Grandpa.

"No, can't say that I have," said Emery thoughtfully.

"Well, that's our escape plan, to build an ice sled."

Grandpa explained that since the Caribou River had just froze over, they should be able to sail down the ice right back to Sawdust Springs. That's if everything goes right. There's often a strong northeast wind blowing down the river in the winter and that's what I'm counting on. ``

"How will you build a sled with that bear wanting to eat us? Asked Emery.

" Well, what I need you and Josh to do is watch out for Single Claw while we're down there working. Here's a whistle. If you see anything, give three long blasts."

"That sounds like a good idea," said Emery, "but we're also going to need some wind if we're going to sail down the river. It's been so still around here that the smoke rises straight up."

"I know," agreed Grandpa. "It's the perfect time to carry out our plan. The lack of wind will make it a lot easier to keep track of Single Claw. Whenever you see the trees or brush move, just blow the whistle. In this part of the country, the north wind could start blowing any time now and we need to be ready when it does."

That afternoon, after Single Claw had left, Grandpa and the grand kids climbed down from the cave and headed toward the icy river which was a short distance away. The snow-covered landscape was silent in the frozen grasp of the far north. Emery and Josh stayed in the cave, keeping the fire burning and keeping a close watch for the bear's return. Grandpa began cutting small trees with his hatchet while the grand kids cut off the limbs and drug them to the frozen river. They formed a small pile of logs at the river's edge.

The Bear Hunters had been working for about an hour, when Josh, scouting from the entrance of the cave, noticed some movement in the brush about a hundred yards north of the work crew. "That must be Single Claw," he thought. "Quick Dad, blow the whistle! That bear is coming back!" he shouted.

Without hesitating, Emery gave three long blasts. He waited a few seconds and then blew the whistle again. He was just about to blow it a third time when Grandpa, and the grandkids came running down the river trail. They had no sooner climbed up the rope into the cave, when Single Claw swatted some saplings aside and roared into the clearing below the cave.

"Good work, Emery," said Grandpa., "Blowing that whistle worked just like we planned! This is what we're going to have to do every time we leave the cave."

Work was slow and dangerous but after three days, they finished the ice sled.

Emery and Josh were grateful for the supply of food the rescuers had brought with them. But there was only enough to last a few more days. They needed to finish the sled and the wind to start blowing. They all knew they wouldn't last long without food in that hostile environment of cold and snow.

The next day our cave dwellers had just finished lunch when Josh pulled out a piece of ivory carved in the shape of a bear. "Look what I found," he said. He held it up so everyone could see.

"Where did you find that?" asked Aria. "That is really unusual!"

"Yeah," said Taven, "I've never seen anything like that before."

"I found it back in the cave the first day we got here," explained Josh.

"Jumping hornytoads!" exclaimed Maddox. "I think you found an old Indian relic. Will you show us where you found it?"

"Sure, follow me," said Josh as he proudly led his curious band of explorers into the darkness toward the back of the cave.

"Wait a minute," said Aria, "I'll grab another candle."

They hadn't gone far when they reached a wall of solid rock. It wasn't a very big cave, but it had kept them warm and sheltered.

"Here's where I found it," pointed Josh. "It was laying right on the surface."

The Bear Hunters got down on their knees and began brushing the loose dirt away, hoping to find some more artifacts. Removing the loose dirt revealed a half dozen arrow heads.

"Wow'!" shouted Josh, "This is amazing!"

Grandpa and Emery headed back in the cave to see what all the excitement was about.

"Look at this grandpa," as Aria held out a hand full of arrowheads.

"Who do you think left this here?" asked Taven.

"Probably some Indians seeking shelter, just like we're doing," answered Grandpa.

They were turning around to leave when the light from William's candle flickered on something. "Wait!" said Maddox, "There's something on the wall." Josh held up his candle too, and sure enough, there was a faded painting of tee pees, canoes, mountains and a river.

"That's called a hieroglyphic," said Emery. "It's an old Indian painting. They were usually done with berry juice and charcoal. It might be hundreds, maybe even thousands of years old."

As Grandpa studied the painting, he explained that this might be the evidence that the lost tribe of the bear Indians tribe inhabited this region years ago.

"There's been a legend about a tribe called the Bear Indians that supposedly lived here about a hundred years ago. For some reason they disappeared, and no one knows why or where they went. This could be the clues to answer those questions. The Bear Indians were said to be a warring tribe and very dangerous. This painting indicates they moved farther north for some unknown reason.

"Wow!" exclaimed Aria. "If Single Claw hadn't chased us up into this cave, who knows when this would have been discovered."

Their discussion was interrupted by a sound coming from outside the cave. "What's that?" asked Jessie. Grandpa cocked his head, cupped his hand behind his ear and then a smile came over his face.

"That's what we've been waiting for. It's the wind coming down the river and the timing is perfect. The north wind is starting to blow!"

CHAPTER 7
THE MIRACLE

"If this wind keeps up," said Grandpa, "we'll leave tomorrow!" Taven and Aria grabbed hands and swung around in circles. Maddox threw his hat in the air and did a cartwheel. They were so excited at the thought of leaving their mountain hideout and heading home.

"What if Single Claw stays around all day and doesn't leave?" asked Josh. "How will we get to the ice sled then?"

"We've got a plan for that," said Aria. "The last time we worked on the sled, we put up a drop net in the trees, just in case we needed to slow that bear down while we reached the sled. We made it out of willow vines."

"How will that work?" asked Josh.

"You'll see," answered Taven. "Well, hopefully, you won't have to see. We don't want that bear chasing us if we can help it."

Then the next morning, a strong, cold, northern wind was blowing down from the mountains. It was a perfect wind for their escape plan.

Grandpa instructed the Bear Hunters to get their weapons ready. He told Emery and Josh to wait and follow them after he gave the signal to leave. Their job was to bring the pup tent Grandpa had brought in his backpack. This would be used for the sail on their ice sled. The kids took turns watching for Single Claw. When he left they would began their escape. Single Claw seemed to sense something was up. He growled and paced back and forth more than usual. Then finally, after several hours, he headed back into the woods to look for food.

"Now's the time!" shouted Maddox. "I just saw Single Claw go into the forest."

"O.K." ordered Grandpa. "Let's go! We've no time to lose."

Grandpa and the Bear Hunters descended down the rope with their weapons ready for action. After scanning the clearing, Grandpa signaled for Emery and Josh to follow. They had just started down the rope with the tent when a thundering roar came from the woods. Emery and Josh stopped and hurried back up the rope. The Bear Hunters had already started down the river trail when they turned and saw Single Claw standing between them and the cave. The bear reared up on his hind legs and let out a blood curdling roar. There was no way now to get past that angry bear to the safety of the cave.

"Take your battle positions!" shouted Grandpa.

Faster than the blink of an eye, the Bear Hunters formed a line of defense. They stood side by side across the trail, facing the killer bear with defiance and courage. Single Claw paused for a moment, not sure of what the Bear Hunters were doing. They weren't running with fear and panic like most due. The bear could sense that these humans were not afraid of him and were ready to fight. Single Claw was more than ready to take them on. He loved to fight! He dropped down on all fours clawing the earth with his long, sharp claws, then charged our brave, young warriors.

"Now Aria!" commanded Grandpa. Aria let fly with one of her arrows and hit the bear right on his bottom. A perfect shot. Single Claw let out a roar and spun around like he'd been stung by a giant bee. When he turned his back for that split second, Taven charged forward with his sword and shield and struck the bear on his side. Single Claw instinctively swatted with his paw and sent him rolling backwards. His shield took most of the blow. When the angry bear started towards Taven, Maddox hurled one of his spears, striking him in the front foot. Roaring with anger, he spun back around. For the first time in his life, Single Claw was totally confused. Every time he made a move, he felt pain. Maddox added more distraction by throwing two of his knives at Single Claw's back feet. The Bear Hunters knew they couldn't kill that bear or even do him much harm, but they could keep him disoriented and confused. They sure were making him dance. Hopefully, he'd get so frustrated he would run back into the woods and leave them alone.

From the safety of the cave, Josh and his dad watched in amazement as four kids and their grandfather fought the largest and meanest bear in the world. Time and again, Single Claw charged, and they would counterattack with a plan of their own. Grandpa directed this little band of warriors like a quarterback leading a football team. Finally, realizing that Single Claw wasn't going to leave, he hollered, "Plan B! Fall back to the drop net!"

The Bear Hunters quickly ran to the edge of the clearing. Single Claw lunged after them, pausing to crouch and grow, hoping to soon finish them off. He was tired of being delayed by their tricky maneuvers. As the angry bear walked under the drop net tied high in the trees above him, Grandpa gave the order.

"Now!"

Aria shot an arrow rope holding the net. A perfect shot sliced the rope in two, dropping the net on top of Single Claw. He thrashed and growled, biting and clawing at the net only to become more entangled.

"Quick!" yelled Grandpa to Emery and Josh., "Run to the river!" They scrambled down the rope carrying the tent and joined the Bear Hunters.

"I don't know how long that net will hold him; he's pretty mad!" panted Grandpa as they ran to the ice sled. They knew they had little time to spare to put up the tent-sail before Single Claw would get away and come after them.

When they reached the frozen river, Grandpa instructed them to shove the sled to the middle of the river. Emery was amazed at how solid and sturdy it was and wondered how they managed to build it with just a hatchet and some rope.

"Hurry, tie the ends of the tent to the mast ropes." shouted Grandpa.

As they hoisted the tent up the mast, the wind filled their homemade sail and slowly began to move the sled. Then something happened that no one expected. The wind died down. In fact, it completely stopped. The sail settled back down like a wrinkled sheet stranding them in the middle of the frozen river. They were helpless without the wind.

"I thought you said the Lord would provide the wind?" said Emery with a sense of panic in his voice.

"That's right," answered Grandpa. "The wind is His department. All we must do is be ready when it comes."

"I hope He decides to send it soon," said Josh. "That bear will be here any minute." The words had no sooner left his mouth when a loud roar came from the river's edge. Single Claw had escaped from the net and was coming out onto the ice towards them.

"Quick, take your battle positions again!" commanded Grandpa.

The Bear Hunters leaped off the sled and formed their defense line again. Their faces were serious. They knew this could be a fight to the end.

There was a metallic "ZZZrring!" as Taven drew his sword from its sheath and held it up in the air. Aria drew back her bow, holding extra arrows in her hand. Maddox held his spear above his shoulder, ready to throw.

Single Claw charged the sled with full fury. When he leaped from the shore onto the ice, his powerful legs sprawled out from under him and he spun in circles, sliding on his belly. The faster he tried to go, the more he slipped and fell, giving precious time for the wind to start blowing again. Finally, the bear managed to slip and slide to within a few yards of them. He was so close they could smell his breath and the bear hunters were just ready to unleash their volley of weapons when Grandpa cried out,

"Lord, if ever we needed wind, we sure do need it now!"

What happened next was nothing short of a miracle.

Suddenly, the sail began to fill with wind as if an angel was blowing on it.

"Hurry, back to the sled!" shouted Grandpa, "The wind is coming!"

The four Bear Hunters turned and dashed back to the sled just as Single Claw charged toward them. When they scampered aboard, a gust of wind hit so hard that it knocked everybody down. Maddox was rolling backwards off the the sled towards Single Claw when Taven grabbed him by the arm and pulled him to safety. Single Claw made one last effort to reach them. He jumped toward the sled but caught only air when the sled took off.

The sled zoomed forward like a shot out of a cannon. In an instant they were up to forty miles an hour, sailing down the middle of the river. The angry bear tried to follow but soon gave up when the sled disappeared around a bend. Grandpa and Emery steered with drag brakes on each side of the sled, just simple sticks that pivoted down against the ice. It was a very effective way to guide the sled.

"Ya hoooo!" yelled Aria. "We're heading home!" Everyone held on tight as the sled flew down the river with amazing speed!

As they raced along, Grandpa looked over at Emery. There was a twinkle in his eye as he said, "Like that old song says, 'God may not come when you want Him, but He's always on time!'"

"I see what you mean," agreed Emery, "He sure is!"

CHAPTER 8

JUSTICE

B ack in Sawdust Springs, the town was still filled with reporters and camera crews. They were waiting for any word about Emery Olson and his son Josh. The whole country was holding its breath, waiting for news of the rescue of one of its wealthiest men.

The favorite gathering spot for the reporters was the dining hall at the Caribou Hotel. It had a beautiful view of the Caribou River. Several people from the media were hanging out there, drinking coffee, discussing current events and waiting for something to happen when Shawn from Fox News saw something on the river. He peered through the window at an object off in the distance coming down the frozen waterway. What was it? He stood up and walked over to the window. This caught the attention of others and soon everyone in the room was standing by the window trying to figure out what it was that they were seeing. When Shawn said, "I think it's some kind of sled with people on board," a stampede started! Grabbing their cameras and computers, they ran to the river's edge, hoping to 'scoop' the first news about the missing fishermen.

When Sheriff Perkins noticed the crowd gathering on the ice behind the hotel, he strode over to see what was going on. Pulling out his binoculars, he studied the small craft that was sailing down the ice and counted seven people on board. He turned to the crowd with a look of satisfaction and said, "Well, my friends, I think our rescue team has finally arrived."

A cheer arose from the crowd.

As the sled got closer, they recognized Emery Olson and his son Josh and cheered again.

Back on the sled, Maddox saw the large crowd standing out on the ice. "Jumping Horny Toads! "What are all those people doing in Sawdust Springs?" Emery, Josh, Grandpa and the Bear Hunters began waving back and shouting to the crowd as they got closer

Cameras were filming this grand event for the whole world to see. When the sled finally reached shore, they were swarmed by reporters. They wanted to know if they were all right, what had happened back on that mountain and how were they rescued? Before Emery Olson would talk to the reporters, he said there was something he wanted to say. He called Grandpa, Aria, Taven and Maddox over to the cameras. "In front of the whole country," Emery introduced them and said, "I want to say thank you to the bravest and best people I've ever met. They're known around these parts as the Bear Hunters. If it hadn't been for these people, Josh and I wouldn't be standing here right now. They saved our lives from the dangerous bear called Single Claw, risking their lives to do it."

Questions were shouted from the crowd and cameras flashed as reporters clambered over each other, trying to get an interview.

That evening when things had settled down, Emery and Josh walked down the snowy road to the little log cabin at the edge of town. They wanted to say good-bye and thank Grandpa and his grandkids again for all they had done for them.

"What a neat little homestead," thought Emery as he knocked on the door. Grandma opened the door and invited the visitors in.

"You must be the two fishermen I've been hearing so much about?" asked Grandma.

"Yes, we are," said Emery. "And we wouldn't be here if your husband and grandkids hadn't rescued us. We wouldn't have survived up there with Single Claw after us."

For the next several hours, everyone sat around the fireplace telling the story of their grand adventure for Grandma. Grandma just shook her head in disbelief at the danger they were in. Grandpa gave an invitation to Emery and Josh to come back and visit anytime they wanted too. Emery said, "Don't be surprised if we take you up on that. We definitely want to keep in touch with you folks."

"That would be nice," said Grandma. "There's something about going through a life-threatening experience that binds people together."

It was hard to say goodbye when the time came.

The next morning, pictures of the Bear Hunters were on the front page of every newspaper in the country. They had received national recognition and put Sawdust Springs on the map. The postmaster worked overtime sorting all the fan mail that began to pour in. Mayor Bud Morgan called for a celebration at the community center to honor their special citizens. A banner was hung over the main street that said, ONCE AGAIN, WE'RE PROUD OF BUCK, ARIA, TAVEN, AND MADDOX.__ THE BEAR HUNTERS OF SAWDUST SPRINGS. The grandkids were proud to have a hometown like Sawdust Springs.

Back in the big city, Emery's brother, Jack Olson, turned on the TV the next morning and gasped. The story of his brother's rescue was breaking news on every major channel. What was he going to do now? It wasn't long before he was mobbed by reporters at his home trying to get an interview. Jack feigned joy over his brothers rescue and said he was happy everything turned out alright.

"This isn't what I planned," thought Jack. "Emery wasn't supposed to survive up there in the wilderness, not with that bear I'd read about."

His plans of being sole owner of the Olson Tractor Company were over. He knew there would be questions about the trip he'd set up for his brother. There would be questions about the article in the *Wilderness Fishing* magazine. If that editor he'd hired talked, it would all be over. Jack's whole world was beginning to unravel.

Sure enough, it wasn't long before the whole truth did come out. The editor confessed and told of an anonymous person paying him big bucks to make up the story. He claimed that if he had known about that killer bear, he never would have written that article. The only thing he knew about the stranger who had paid him the money was that he had a briefcase with the initials 'J.O.' on it.

Of course, the authorities pieced the puzzle together and traced the initials to Jack Olson. After intense questioning by the police, Jack confessed. He said he wanted to be sole owner of the business. That's why he set up the fishing trip after reading about a killer bear on the Caribou River. He was charged with attempted murder and placed in custody while awaiting trail.

Emery Olson had a hard time believing that his brother would do such a thing. How could anyone be filled with so much envy and bitterness that they would take another person's life, especially their own brother?

It had been a hard year for Emery. He'd lost his wife and now his brother. He put his arm around his son's shoulder, and the two slowly walked away from the jail where Jack was confined. Turning to Josh, he said, "I guess I should have done more. All my life I tried to deal with my brother's jealousy by ignoring it and hoping it would go away. At times I thought he'd gotten past it but now I know it was always there, just under the surface. What Jack did was wrong, giving us a good gift with such bad intentions. What I want to do is look for some good that could come from all of this. I want Jack to know that I still love him as a brother and forgive him. My main concern is that he gets some help. Who knows, maybe after rehabilitation and counseling, some day he could come back to the business. You know, I've been thinking it's about time you and I find a church and get serious about our walk with the Lord. We need to learn more about that miracle wind that saved us up there on that frozen river. Or should I say how God saved us from that bear they call Single Claw!"

STORY FIVE

GHOST DRUMS ON THE CARIBOU

It's been said the most rugged and unexplored land in the world is not the jungles, the deserts or the rivers of the lower latitudes, but the barrens of the far north where thousands of miles of desolate planet have yet to feel the footprint of man. A land full of extremes where temperatures range from 90 above to 90 below. A contrast of light and darkness where the sun barely sets for half the year and then refuses to rise for the other half. If ever there is a place where one could disappear from civilization, it's the inhospitable and dangerous barrens of the far north.

CHAPTER 1

MIRACLE AT CANYON CREEK

The weathered old prospector crouched at the side of the creek, panning for gold. Each swirl of the pan promised wealth and fortune that had eluded him for years. The day was almost gone when he heard a twig snap behind him. A grizzly bear. A very large grizzly was watching him. Before he could turn around the bear was on him, tearing and ripping his clothes and flesh with lightning speed. The mauling lasted only a few seconds and then the gigantic bear bounded back into the woods. The injured prospector dragged himself over to his donkey, slumped over its back and headed for help.

———◄◄❁►►———

Sheriff Perkins had just finished his coffee and started down the cold boardwalk of Sawdust Springs, making his morning rounds. He pulled his collar up around his neck as even in June, the mornings have an icy bite in the far north. That's when he noticed a donkey at the far end of the street standing over a clump of something. When the donkey saw him, it started baying. As he got closer, he realized the clump he saw was a body. He rushed over to discover a short, stocky man lying in a heap where he'd collapsed at the north end of town. Who he was, where he'd come from and how long he'd laid there were all a mystery. The old man looked more dead than alive. His full scruffy beard, leathery skin, and thick callused hands were the typical appearance of those who hunt for gold. His faithful donkey stood by his side baying for help. Sheriff Perkins knelt down and checked for a pulse. He was still alive!

"Quick, go get Doc Barns!" he yelled at Pete McCormic who had just come out of the hardware store. "I've got an injured man here!"

A crowd of curious onlookers soon gathered, waiting for the town's doctor to arrive. The Sheriff gently placed his hand under the old man's head and carefully rolled him over.

"Hang in their Old Timer, the Doc is on his way."

The old man slowly opened his eyes and whispered in a faint voice, "Am I still alive?"

"You sure are," grinned the sheriff. "Somehow you made it to Sawdust Springs. From the looks of things, you've tangled with one whopper of a bear."

He looked up and nodded in agreement and then mumbled something about drums, drums beating in the distance, then lost consciousness again.

It wasn't long before Doc Barns arrived at the scene and made his way through the crowd of curious onlookers. Opening his black leather bag, he took out his stethoscope and checked for a pulse.

"Everyone be quiet!" Instructed the Doc. "He's got such a faint heartbeat; I can barely hear it." Silence fell over the crowd and after a quick examination, Doc gave orders to bring him to his office.

"Where do you suppose he came from?" asked Doc Barns.

Sheriff Perkins shook his head. "I'm not sure but from the direction he entered town, he must have come from Bear Mountain." He then gave orders to some of the by-standers to take the old man's donkey down to the livery stable and tell Jake to take good care of it. The town will pay the bill.

Grandpa and his three grandkids, Aria, Taven and Maddox were feeding their horses when Sheriff Perkins entered the barn. The children were staying with their grandparents while their parents went down to the states to buy supplies for their new store. They had just purchased the hardware store and moved up to Sawdust Springs last year.

"Hello Sheriff," greeted Grandpa. "What brings you over so early in the morning?"

The sheriff explained how he'd found an old man passed out at the north end of town while making his morning rounds. "It was a good thing I came across him when I did, He wouldn't have lasted much longer without the doc's help. Looks like some bear got a hold of him and tore him up pretty bad. You don't often see men go through what he did and live to tell about it!"

"Who was it?" asked Grandpa.

Sheriff Perkins shook his head. "I don't know, I've never seen him before. He's not able to answer any questions right now. That's why I was hoping you would come over to Doc's office and see if you might recognize him."

"That's sure strange?" said Aria. "Doesn't anyone know where he came from or how he wound up at Sawdust Springs?"

"No, like I said, he's too weak to talk. Probably a prospector working a claim up on Bear Mountain. That would be my guess. He does keep mumbling something about drums though. Don't have a clue as to what that means."

"Drums?" asked Maddox. "You mean like Indian drums?"

"Who knows. It's all a mystery to me." answered the Sheriff. "That's why I was hoping your grandpa would come down to Doc's office to help us find some answers."

"Sure, I'll come," said Grandpa, "In fact, we'll all come."

The grand kids laid down their tools and followed Sheriff Perkins and Grandpa over to Doc Barns office. When they saw the condition of the injured man, Taven let out a gasp. "Wow, it is a wonder he's still alive."

"It sure is," agreed the Doc. "He's wrestled with an ornery bear alright, that's for sure."

Grandpa nodded his head. "He's mighty fortunate to survive such a terrible mauling. And from the pattern of the claw marks, Single Claw was responsible for this."

"Jumping horny toads," said Maddox, "you're right. There's just one lone claw mark on most of his body."

"Boy, that one sure slipped by me," said Sheriff Perkins, "I didn't notice the single claw marks. Well, what do you think, Buck, have you ever seen him before?" (Buck was Grandpa's nickname that the town's people knew him by.)

Grandpa shook his head. "No, I don't think so. I've never laid eyes on him, but from the extent of his injuries it would be hard for anyone to recognize him."

They were all surprised when the old man began to move. He opened his eyes and spoke in a low whisper voice, "Drums.......drums saved my life."

"That's what he keeps saying," said the Sheriff. "Something about drums saving his life. Got any idea what that might mean?"

"Well, my guess is, he's probably just hallucinating," answered the Doc. "I'll be sure and notify you when he comes to."

"That would be great." said the Sheriff, "This one really got me baffled. I'll give you a call too Buck, if you want?"

"You bet," said Grandpa. "I'll be glad to help anyway I can."

On the way back to the ranch Maddox was in deep thought.

"I was just thinking. If it was Single Claw that did this, how could he have survived? Not many people live through an attack from that killer bear."

"Yeah," said Taven, "That's a good question. Maybe there is something about drums that saved him, but I don't see how."

"That's what I was thinking," said Maddox. "How could drums save anyone from a bear attack, especially Single Claw?"

"Well,"said Aria, "We'll just have to wait until he gets better to find out what really happened. We could speculate till the cows come home but it won't do us any good. Besides, we've got chores to do."

They all knew she was right. Being the oldest, Aria always looked at things in a more grownup way.

———————)❦(——————

Four days later, while everyone was enjoying one of Grandma's famous chicken and dumpling dinners, the phone rang. Grandpa shoved away from the table and ambled over to the phone.

"Hello," —— "I'm doing fine, Doc, how's your new patient doing?"

"He seems to be doing better, answered Doc. "He's awake now and talking a little. Sheriff Perkins had to go out of town for a couple days and ask me to call you if he woke up while he's away. He's hoping you can help figure out what happened. Can you come down to my office?

"You bet I'll come," responded Grandpa. "I'm just finishing dinner and then I'll be right over." Grandpa wiped his face, picked up his hat and walked over to the front door. After putting on his coat he paused and turned around with a questioning smile.

"Well, who wants to come with me?" There was a small stampede as all three Grand kids scrambled from the table and ran for their coats faster than a fly from a swatter.

"We were hoping we could come," said Aria.

"Well, I don't see why not." answered Grandpa. "After all, this was a bear attack. It only seems right that the 'bear hunters' should be involved." That was the name given them after all their close encounters with Single Claw.

The kids were so excited that they practically ran all the way to Doc Barn's office, tugging Grandpa by the hand. When they finally arrived, Doc thanked them for coming and led them to the back room. He gave instructions not to stay too long since his patient was still very weak and needed to conserve energy for recuperating.

When they entered the room, they were amazed at the old man's progress.

"Wow," said Jessie, "You sure have improved since we last saw you."

He turned slowly and spoke in a soft voice, "I must not have looked too hunky dory from the sound of things."

"You sure didn't," said Grandpa. "Doc has done a fine job of patching you back together."

The old man felt the bandages on his head and asked, "How in tarnation did I get here in the first place."

"Sheriff Perking found you at the edge of town where you fell off your donkey."

The old man's eyes widened. "Maybell! Where's Maybell?" he asked.

"You mean your donkey?" asked Grandpa. "She's down at the livery stable and being well cared for." The old man gave a sigh of relief.

"We weren't sure anyone in your shape would pull through." said Taven.

"Most people wouldn't," chimed in Doc. "He's as tough as a rattlesnake to pull through like he did."

"And don't forget, I'm as ornery as one too," the old man said with a smile.

"Excuse me for not introducing myself." said Grandpa. "They call me Buck." He paused a second, "Or Grandpa. Whichever you prefer."

"Mine is Calhoon, Cactus Calhoon."

Grandpa's eyes widened. "So, you're Cactus Calhoon! I think everyone in the far north has heard about you. You're a legend when it comes to prospectors, trappers and mountain men. It's a real pleasure to finally meet you."

"The pleasure's all mine," said Cactus, "I just wish it had been under better circumstances."

"I know," said Grandpa. "Do you feel up to telling us what happened? If you don't, we'll understand, we can come back another time."

"No, now's as good a time as any," said Cactus. "I'll bet the whole town is hankerin to hear why an old beat-up prospector drug up on their doorstep."

"Well, we were wondering," said Maddox. "You've been unconscious for four days and we've been anxiously waiting to find out."

Cactus rubbed his beard. "I'll be a sorry sidewinder. I had no idea I was out for that long."

"You sure were," said Doc. "I'm glad to see you're doing better. What happened to you anyway? You've been mumbling something about distant drums saving your life ever since we brought you in here."

Cactus stared at the ceiling as he pulled his thoughts together. "The last I recall; I was crouched down working my gold pan up on Canyon Creek. That's where my claim is. I turned around when I heard a noise and that's when I saw the largest, con-founded bar I've ever seen, charging likadee split right at me. I didn't have time to even think before that ornery cuss was on me. He bushwhacked me quicker than a chicken on a June bug. I was flung in the air and tossed around like a rag doll. After several seconds of this, that bar stood up on his hind legs, towering over me like a giant oak tree. He raised his paw for one final swipe. A creature that size could easily rip you in two and I was sure I was a goner. I closed my eyes expecting to meet my maker, and that's when I heard it."

"Heard what?" interrupted a wide-eyed Aria.

"Ghost drums," said Cactus, "The ghost drums on the Caribou River. The steady; 'Boom, boom, boom, boom,' coming from somewhere off in the distance.

"Ghost drums!" Exclaimed Taven, "What in the world is that?"

Cactus Calhoon looked surprised.

"You mean you've never heard of the ghost drums? Well, the legend goes that when an Indian is killed by a bear, his spirit comes back to warn others when a dangerous bear is around. They try to scare the bear off by beating the ghost drums."

"Do you believe that"? asked Maddox, "There's no such thing as a ghost."

"I sure do, they saved my life, by cracky! This isn't the first time I've heard them either. Twice before when the moon was full and the wind was coming from the north, I heard them on the back side of Bear Mountain. When that old bar charged me, I was so scared, I thought at first the drums were my own heart pounding, but then I noticed that the bar heard it too. I was shocked when he stood up and then froze like a giant statue trying to figure out where the ghost drums were coming from. Sniffing the air for a scent, he finally dropped down on all fours and lunged off into the woods running toward those tom-toms. I tell you, them, thar drums saved my life. I laid there for a while playing dead and when I realized he wasn't coming back. I struggled to climb up on Maybell's back and we started out of the mountains. I knew I was hurt purty bad and wouldn't last long without help. Don't know how far or how long I traveled but the next recollection I have is waking up here at Doc's office this evening."

"Well, I'll tell you how far you made it," said Doc. "You made it all the way to Sawdust Springs. Sheriff Perkins found you laying in the middle of the road just outside of town."

The old man shook his head in disbelief. "Why that's two to three days travel from where my claim is up on Canyon Creek. How in tarnation could I have made it that far? Must of lost conciseness and Maybell just kept going"

"I don't know," answered Doc, "but like I said, you'd have to be pretty tough to live through what you did and then travel that distance with the injuries you had."

"Sounds to me like the good Lord had his hand in this," responded Grandpa.

Cactus nodded his head in agreement.

"That's the strangest story I've ever heard," interrupted Aria.

"Me too," said Maddox. "You're sure fortunate to be alive."

Cactus was starting to doze off again. Grandpa was about to ask more questions when Doc interrupted him. "I think my patient could use a little rest about now. They'll be plenty of time for more questions later." Everyone knew Doc was right and quietly slipped out of his office.

Grandpa and his grandkids talked about the mystery of the drums as they walked back home in the moonlight. "For some reason Single Claw was distracted by the sound of drums," said Aria.

"I know," said Taven. "Why would Single Claw give a hoot about any drums? He's normally only worked up over campfires."

"Yeah, but aren't you forgetting something?" asked Maddox. The most important question is, where did those drums come from in the first place? We don't think ghost were involved, do we?"

"No ," said Grandpa, "we don't. It must have been real Indians but there's just one problem."

"And what's that, asked Aria?"

"There haven't been any Indians in these parts for close to a hundred years."

CHAPTER 2

Mystery Drums

Grandpa was working on the corral gate when he heard the kids arguing about something out behind the barn.

"I think it runs east, up this valley."

"Well, I don't, I think it comes from this valley, further to the west."

"You're both wrong. It stays close to the Caribou River and then forks off in this direction."

Grandpa came around the barn and saw his three Grandkids on their hands and knees drawing lines in the dirt with sticks.

"What do we have here, an artist convention? What's all the arguing about?"

The three children turned around and looked up from their scratches in the soft barn yard dirt.

"Oh, hi Grandpa," said Aria. "We were just making maps on which way we think Canyon Creek flows into the Caribou River."

"Sounds like a pretty intense discussion to me." said Grandpa. "Why all the interest in Canyon Creek anyway?"

"Well," said Taven, "We were just trying to figure out where Cactus Calhoon's claim was. That's where he was panning gold when Single Claw attacked him."

"Yeah," said Maddox, "That's where he heard the drums."

"And we were just thinking, we might hear them too if we went to his claim," added Aria.

"Oh, now I see," said Grandpa as he wiped his brow. "I'm starting to get the picture. You're wanting to use those drums as an excuse to go on another adventure, aren't you?"

"I guess you could put it that way," said Aria. "The way we see it, there can only be three explanations to Cactus Calhoon's story.

"And what might they be?" asked Grandpa.

"Well, the first one is, he was hallucinating. He really didn't hear anything at all," said Taven.

"Then the second one," added Maddox, "There are things that make noises like a drum. Like a woodpecker pounding on a hollow log, or a tree caught in the river bouncing against a rock in the current."

"Then, the third one," said Aria, " He really did hear actual Indian drums."

"Aren't you forgetting another possibility?" asked Grandpa.

"What's that?" They all said in unison.

"What about the old Indian legend of the 'Ghost Drums'!" Grandpa said with a grin.

"Oh Grandpa, we're serious. We know you don't really believe in ghost….do you?" asked Maddox.

215

"No, of course not. I'm just pulling your leg. But I am curious, what do you think caused those drums? Was it hallucinations, woodpeckers, or Indians?"

They looked at each other with raised shoulders.

"Well," said Aria, "We thought that if there was any chance at all there might be Indians living on the back side of Bear Mountain, it would sure be a great discovery to find them."

"And you want to go on a wild goose chase that's probably hallucinations of a battered old prospector?" asked Grandpa. "I hate to put a damper on your adventure, but you need more evidence than that. Remember, there hasn't been any sign of Indians living in these parts for a long, long time."

As the grand kids were trying to convince Grandpa of the possibility of Indians living in the uninhabited wilderness north of Bear Mountain, a familiar sound filled the air.

"Hee Haw, Hee Haw." Then a loud mournful howl of a blood hound.

"Ham Bone and Conniption," shouted Maddox. "Yea, Rawhide Jake is here!" yelled Taven.

Coming down the trail they could see Rawhide Jake leading his little donkey, Conniption, with Ham Bone, the best hound dog in the world walking by his side. Rawhide was the only person in the territory that homesteaded on the back side of Bear Mountain. Every year in the Spring, he comes to town for supplies and to visit his friends.

The kids ran to greet their visitors and after hugging Rawhide, switched their attention to the animals. They threw their arms around them and smothered them with affection. Hambone's tongue, as usual, was licking faster than a machine gun, cleaning the dust from the children's faces. Conniption bowed his head as the kids rubbed behind his ears. Those two little animals loved the grandchildren, and the kids loved them.

"It's sure great to see you again," said Grandpa. "I figured you'd be coming for supplies soon after the spring thaw a couple weeks ago. Supper will be ready in a little while and as you know, there's always a place for you to spread your bedroll up in the hay loft.

Rawhide looked forward to their hospitality and a chance to catch up on all the latest news. Later that evening, the children put Conniption in the stable and gave him a generous portion of hay. Hambone was allowed to come inside and sleep on the braided rug in front of the fireplace. After washing up, they all sat down and enjoyed one of Grandma's wonderful, home cooked dinners of okra with fried grits, hush puppies, biscuits and gravy, corn on the cob and skillet fried chicken. Enough to feed a King's banquet. She still used the old Monarch, wood fired, cook stove Grandpa had bought her when they first got married. They ate so much they thought they were going to pop.

"That was a wonderful dinner," Rawhide said to Grandma as she took his plate from the table. After everyone was finished, they all gathered in the living room in front of the fireplace where Hambone was sprawled out. Taven laid down beside the old hound dog, rubbing his belly. Nothing could beat a crackling fire, a full meal and listening to Grandpa and Rawhide swap stories.

It wasn't long before Grandpa mentioned the bear attack that happened to the old prospector up on Canyon creek and how fortunate he was to be alive.

"Who was it?" asked Rawhide. "Is he going to pull through?"

"Sure looks like it." said Grandpa. "It was that legend of a mountain man, Cactus Calhoon!"

"Cactus Calhoon! Exclaimed Rawhide. "Why, I haven't seen that old tumbleweed in a dog's year. That's seven years to you younguns, if you didn't know."

"Well, we can take you to him in the morning," said Grandpa. "He's recouping at Doc Barn's place after that awful mauling."

"You bet," said Aria. "We were just talking about him when you arrived. You see, Grandpa doesn't believe, and we want too."

"Believe what?" asked Rawhide.

"The story about Indian drums distracting Single Claw and saving Mr. Calhoon's life.

Grandpa thinks he was just delirious from being mauled." said Maddox

"And what do you believe?" asked Rawhide.

"We're not sure," answered Aria, "but we were thinking that an expedition to find out would be a great adventure. Have you ever heard of any Indians drums in your travels around Bear Mountain?"

Rawhide paused as he reached down and petted Hambone. It seemed like a minute passed before he finally spoke. All ears were at attention.

"As a matter of fact,...... I have."

Grandpa's eyes widened and the children scooted closer so they wouldn't miss a word. All eyes focused on Rawhide.

"Well, what I'm about to tell you, I've not told another soul." began Rawhide. "You see, most people wouldn't believe me anyhow, but since you brought it up, here's where I think those drums are coming from. He leaned forward and whispered in a quiet, suspenseful voice, "It's the ghost drums from the spirits of the dead."

"Jumping horny toads," exclaimed Maddox, "that's what Cactus Calhoon said too!"

"That's right." exclaimed Taven. "He said it was an old Indian legend."

"It is," agreed Rawhide, "When the moon is full and the night is as black as coal, the spirits of Indians that were killed by bears began to beat the ghost drums. They're warning others when a bear is watching in the darkness, waiting for the right moment to attack. When a bear hears the ghost drums, the legend says they run with fear trying to get away." Rawhide was enjoying every minute of his wild tale.

The children didn't say a word as they starred with wide eyes at Rawhide.

"Now don't let me scare you," consoled Rawhide, "There might just be another explanation. Besides, I'm not so sure I believe in ghost anyway."

Grandpa was relieved to hear that and added, "Well we sure don't."

The children nodded in agreement.

"What's your other explanation then for the drums?" asked Aria.

"Simple," said Rawhide, "It's real Indians beating real drums. It doesn't make a campfire story near as suspenseful, but it does make a lot of sense."

"What makes you think that?" asked Grandpa

"You see, the way I've figure it," begin Rawhide, "About 100 years ago, the Bear Indians suddenly disappeared from these parts. Some say it was a smallpox epidemic that wiped them out. Others think it was lack of food because of several bad winters that drove them away. Whatever it was, they're no longer here. I always thought they went further south where the climate wasn't so harsh. Then, one cold autumn evening, when I was prospecting way up on the Caribou River, I heard their drums. It sent chills up my spine, it did. A full moon was coming up and a gentle breeze was blowing from the north. Usually, the wind always comes from the south but this time it was blowing right down the river. Sound can carry a lot farther over water.

"What did you do then?" asked Aria.

"Well," continued Cactus, "Not much I could do sep listen. I heard them fer about fifteen minutes and then they quit. I thought of the possibility right then and thar that the Bear Indians could have settled north of Bear Mountain, beyond the Valley of No Return where the desolate Barrens stretch for miles.

"The Barrens?" asked Taven, "I've never heard of them before."

Rawhide sat back in the rocking chair with a cup of coffee in his hand. " The Barrens are probable the most rugged and inhospitable place in the world. Miles and miles of frozen wasteland that few people have ever seen. You can't even see it from a plane. Pilots have told me there's a heavy fog vapor that hangs constantly over the land. If a person wanted to hide from the world, that's the place to be."

"How far north of Bear Mountain are the Barrens?" asked Aria.

"A good week's travel." answered Rawhide. "Just beyond the 'Valley of No Return'."

"The Valley of No Return! That sounds scarry." gasped Maddox. "Why do they call it that?"

"Cause them foolish enough to try and cross it, seldom come back. You see, that valley extends north as far as the frozen arctic. There's a north wind that blows down through it that causes a severe and drastic weather change. It's like night and day. The temperature can drop from a hot summer day of 80 degrees to 60 below zero in the middle of that valley. If you aren't prepared for it you'll freeze to death quicker than it takes to tell about it."

"Yes," said Grandpa, "And if there are real Indians living on the other side of that valley, it could be another reason few ever come back from the Barrens. They might not be too friendly to the idea of being discovered."

The mystery of the drums consumed the conversation until it was time to hit the hay.

The children could hardly sleep that night with the thought of a search party for the lost tribe of the Bear Indians. Now, all they had to do was convince Grandpa. That would be the hard part.

By the end of the week, Rawhide Jake had finished gathering his needed supplies. He loaded up everything and was ready to head back to his cabin on the far side of Bear Mountain. This time, he would be taking with him a special passenger; Cactus Calhoon and his donkey, Maybell! Rawhide had invited Cactus to come stay with him until he fully recovered from his bear attack. Doc Barns thought it was a wonderful idea and encouraged his patient to take the offer. The two would be a perfect match since they would have more stories to share than a dog has fleas.

Grandma packed a batch of buttermilk biscuits for Rawhide and Cactus to eat on the way. They exchanged their goodbyes and Grandpa extended an open invitation to them whenever they came to town. Two, old scruffy prospectors, two donkeys and a hound dog, slowly headed into the magnificent wilderness of Bear Mountain. An occasional Hee-Haw could be heard off in the distance from Maybell as she was so happy to be reunited with Cactus Calhoon once again.

CHAPTER 3

THE SEARCH BEGINS

G randpa called out, "Who wants to go to town for supplies?"

The Grand kids came out of the barn where they had been brushing down their horses.

"Supplies?" asked Aria, "Didn't you pick up supplies a couple days ago?"

"I sure did but wouldn't it be foolish to take off on another adventure without being properly prepared." answered Grandpa.

The kids couldn't believe what they just heard. It had been a week of arm-twisting Grandpa to go searching for the Bear Indians. They had tried every trick in the book to sway him and he appeared unbudgeable.

"Do you mean we're going to search for the lost tribe of the Bear Indians?" asked Taven.

"Well, I've thought it over and if you're right. It would be one the greatest discoveries of the far north. To find that lost tribe," said Grandpa.

"Jumping horny toads!" shouted Maddox, "We're really going?"

"Yes," said Grandpa, "I just couldn't get it out of my mind. I finally convinced your grandma, and myself, that if we prepare properly and take all the safety precautions, we'll have a wonderful, safe trip. And who knows, we might just add a page to history about the missing Indians."

The air was buzzing with excitement as preparations got under way.

Grandpa checked and double checked his list to make sure they didn't forget anything.

Grandma helped with the food and warm cloths.

"Grandpa, why are we packing our warm arctic cloths? It's summer and hot." asked Aria.

"Just a precaution encase that story Cactus Calhoon told us about a freezing valley is true." answered Grandpa.

The children made sure they packed their weapons for self-defense. Taven had his sword and shield, Aria had her bow and arrows, And Maddox had his throwing knives and spear. No one in the country could handle these weapons better than the Bear Hunters. Every day they practiced for at least an hour and Grandpa said they were so good they could easily win a gold medal in the Olympics. The decision was made to leave the horses behind on this trip since they would be going through unknown territory that could require some mountain climbing.

It took three days preparing for the trip before they rounded up everything they needed. Grandpa had just one thing left to do for a safety precaution; notify Sheriff Perkins about their destination and estimated return time.

They were now ready to begin their search for the lost tribe of the Bear Indians.

The morning was warm and clear on the day of their departure. Snowcapped Bear Mountain stood majestically in the distance adorned by fluffy white clouds and a lone, soaring eagle. The smell of pine trees filled the air as Blue Jays chattered from branch to branch. As far as the residents of Sawdust Springs were concerned, there wasn't a more picturesque place in the whole world than the far north.

"I can't believe we're actually doing this," said Aria. "This is a rare expedition since we're not saving someone's life. Not that I mind doing that. This is just more like a vacation, that's all."

"I know," said Grandpa. "Not having to worry about rescuing someone from Single Claw, like we normally do, will be quite different."

A nagging thought came to Grandpa, 'If only this would be true.'

After bowing their heads for a time of prayer to ask God's blessing and protection on their trip, the explorers headed off. They left Sawdust Springs at mid-morning in high spirits. As always, their first stop will be the campsite at Sawdust Springs Ranger Station

at Loon Lake about five miles north of town. They could easily make more distance than that, but this gave them an opportunity to catch and release some of the huge fish Loon Lake is famous for. They loved to sit around the evening campfire and listen to the haunting calls of the loons echoing across the water. Sometimes, tradition and memories are more important than mileage.

Besides, the next leg of the journey would consist of steep elevation gains as they headed into the high country of Bear Mountain. They wanted to be fresh and rested before starting that climb. Also, from here on out, there won't be any campfires because they'll be in Single Claw country and there's nothing that makes that bear madder than a campfire. It reminds him of the forest fire years ago that burned off all the claws of his right paw, except one.

The next morning, breakfast was served at the crack of dawn.

"Rise and shine you sleepy heads," shouted Grandpa, "We're wasting daylight!

Everyone cheerfully jumped out of their sleeping bags, ready for the days adventure. They had learned from a young age that the attitude you wake up with is just a habit so you might as well be cheerful instead of grouchy.

After a hearty breakfast of Bannock and pemmican, they broke camp and headed further into the northern wilderness.

"Grandpa," Asked Taven, "Have you heard anything about Single Claw recently? He's been mighty quiet after he attacked Cactus Calhoon."

"I know," answered Grandpa, "but we don't want to let our guard down. That's when accidents happen. We'll still keep our campfires out and be on the alert."

The going was ruff and required frequent rest stops. It would take two days to get past Bear Mountain and then five more days of hard hiking to make it to the Barrens where the 'Valley of No Return' was supposed to be.

Maddox was concerned about going through a valley with such a dreadful name.

"Are you sure we'll be alright going into that frozen wasteland."

Grandpa reassured him that with their goose down parka's, they'd be as comfortable as a chick under their mother's wings.

"Don't you worry about going through that valley," encouraged Grandpa. "Remember, Catus Calhoon said it was those that weren't prepared that had all the trouble. That's why we took special precautions packing all our supplies. Especially the winter gear even though it's still summer."

Day three of their six-day journey brought them to the confluence of the Caribou River and Canyon Creek.

"This looks like the place where Cactus Calhoon had his mining claim," said Grandpa. "It might have been right here on this very gravel bar that Single Claw attacked him."

"You're right," said Taven, "And there's his gold pan over by that log."

The kids ran and picked it up.

Aria's eyes widened. "Look at this. Teeth marks where Single Claw bit it."

"Wow," said Maddox, "We should take it back as a souvenir for Cactus Calhoon. I'm sure he'd like to have this for a show and tell when spinning yarns with his old buddies."

They decided to make camp for the night at the same place where Cactus said he heard the ghost drums. Their hopes were high with anticipation that they too would hear the drums, but the night passed without a sound. Early the next morning Taven was the first to wake up.

He was as disappointed as the others when they didn't hear the ghost drums and then he remembered an old hollow log he'd seen stuck in a sand bar at Canyon creek. Quietly slipping out of his sleeping bag he picked up a stick and went down to beat the hollow log. Boom.... boom boom boom, Boom....boom boom boom came the sound of drums in the early, misty dawn.

Maddox bolted out of his sleeping bag. "Jumping Horny Toads, It's the Ghost Drums!"

Within seconds everyone was up and listening.

"See, what did I tell you. They're real." Maddox said to Grandpa.

Aria rubbed her eyes as she sat up listening. Their minds where whirling with excitement at the sound of the ghost drums.

After a couple of minutes Taven, hiding around the bend in the river, couldn't hold it any longer and burst out with loud laughter.

"Where was Taven?" thought Grandpa, as he noticed he wasn't at the campsite. And then a smile began to creep over his face.

"You're right," Grandpa said, "They are for real. But I never knew that Indians laughed just like Taven when they play their drums."

Taven came around the sandbar with a stick in his hand bent over with laughter. When the others realized they had been duped, a slow rage began to rise.

"Why, of all the low-down dirty tricks." shouted Aria. "How could you do that? You really had us going."

Aria and Maddox held a quick huddle and decided that the best payback for Taven would be a quick dunk in the icy creek. They started chasing him when something happened that brought them all to a halt. Two large grizzly bears charged out from the trees and out onto the river bar. They were puzzled and surprised when they saw the campers and skidded to an abrupt stop. The bears were sniffing the air and looking for something. After a few minutes of not finding what they were looking for, they turned and ran back into the woods.

"Did you see that?" shouted Aria.

"I sure did," answered Grandpa. "Those bears were looking for something and I think the sound of Taven's drums is what brought them to us. Taven, your little practical joke has given us a clue for the reason of those ghost drums."

"Like what?" asked Maddox, "What were they looking for?"

"I don't know," said Grandpa. "But there is definitely a connection with the sound of drums and those bears. Just what it is I don't know but they sure were looking for something when Taven began beating on that log. We need to test this theory further about the connection between drums and bears but for now we better keep moving if we're going to make it to the Barrens on schedule."

Taven drew a sigh of relief, for just in a matter of minutes, he had turned from an object of reprisal and ridicule to a hero.

That day they traveled further north of Bear Mountain than they had ever been before. The scenery was beautiful, and the weather was sunny and warm. There couldn't have been a better day for hiking through the mountains.

The call of ravens and majestic eagles souring in the mountain skies added the perfect touch to a beautiful day.

"How far are we going today?" asked Aria.

Grandpa looked at the horizon. "You see that flat plateau beyond the hills. Let's try to make it that far. From the directions Rawhide gave, the 'Valley of No Return' shouldn't be far from there."

Grandpa knew it was good to have a daily destination for a goal. It gave everyone extra incentive. By evening they had reached the plateau just as it was getting dark. There was just enough twilight left to set up camp. They were all tuckered out and settled on dry beef jerky for dinner rather than preparing a big meal. Extreme fatigue had taken away their appetite. Sleep came almost instantly when they crawled into their sleeping bags. About an hour had passed when Grandpa was the first to hear it! The sound of drums coming from the far north!

"Wake up every one!" shouted Grandpa. "It's the drums!"

The children were so groggy, Grandpa had a hard time waking them up. When they did, excitement filled the air.

"It's real, It's real!" shouted Taven. "I'm not doing it this time."

"We know silly." said Aria. "I can't believe we're actually hearing the ghost drums." She paused for a moment. "Or whatever kind of drums they are!"

"Wow Grandpa!" said Maddox, "This makes it all worth it, doesn't it?"

"You bet," said Grandpa. "I'm glad I changed my mind about coming."

The drums only lasted for about fifteen minutes and then stopped. They heard the sound of a bear crashing through the brush running toward the drums. Then, all was quiet.

Their minds were whirling with questions of why and who was beating those drums.

"Finally, we heard them, we really heard them." said Aria. "We're no longer on a wild goose chase."

"You're right," said Grandpa. "But there's nothing more we can do tonight. We'd better try and get some sleep. We can talk about this in the morning. We're going to have a big day tomorrow if we find the 'Valley of No Return' and we're going to need all the rest we can get." As hard as it was, they finally quit talking and drifted back to sleep.

CHAPTER 4

THE VALLEY OF NO RETURN

When the sun came up and morning mist cleared from the high plateau, their eyes couldn't believe what they saw. The dim rising sun illuminated a deep gorge lying just ahead of them.

"Wow," exclaimed Aria, "Is that the 'valley of no return'?"

Grandpa cleaned his glasses for a better look.

"It must be." answered Grandpa. "The description matches what we've heard." A long, wide valley just ahead of the barrens."

Taven wondered why it was so dangerous since it didn't seem that wide. Maybe just two miles at the widest point.

"Jumping horny toads," shouted Maddox. "I don't see why they call it the 'valley of no return'. Why we could make it across in about a half hour easily."

Grandpa studied the valley carefully.

"I think I have the answer to that. How warm is it today?"

"About 65 degrees right now, and it's supposed to get up to around 75 or 80." answered Maddox. "What does that have to do with making the valley so dangerous."

"Take a close look on the other side." said Grandpa. "What do you see."

They all strained their eyes to try and see what Grandpa saw.

"All I see," said Aria, "is some sort of fog on the far side of the valley. It looks like the land is covered with thick clouds."

"That's right," responded Grandpa. "If I'm right, that's no ordinary fog, but a freezing fog from a drastic temperature change. And from the way it's moving there's a strong wind blowing as well."

"Remember what Cactus Calhoon told us about a valley that changes temperature so much that people freeze to death trying to cross it? Well, I think this is that valley. 'The Valley of No Return'!

"How could that be?" asked Taven. "It's so warm over here and there's not a breath of wind at all."

"Well, it's my guess that this is the valley that cuts right up into the northern Arctic and acts like a funnel for the extreme cold to travel down through it. I'll bet it's freezing in the middle of that valley."

"So that's why people are caught unprepared when then try to cross it?" asked Maddox.

Grandpa nodded his head. "That's right. This could be one of those strange weather inversions I've read about where there is a drastic temperature change. So, what I want us all to do when we get closer, before we climb down into that valley and begin our crossing, is to put on our insulated arctic cloths that we brought."

"But Grandpa," questioned Aria, "It's way too hot to put on cloths like that. We'll sweat like little pigs."

"Oink! Oink!" Squealed Maddox. "That's alright, there one of the smartest animals on earth, so I don't mind imitating them with a little sweat."

Grandpa gave all the children a stern look. "If I'm wrong, we can quickly take them off. But if I'm right, we'll be mighty glad we put them on. They could save our lives!"

After having breakfast and breaking camp, they headed toward the fog covered valley. Everyone put on their warm winter cloths before starting down the plateau for the valley crossing. Grandpa had them tie themselves together with rope to insure no one got separated and lost.

"Boy am I hot." complained Taven.

"Me too," moaned the other children.

They waddled off like a flock of pin quins in their bulky parkas as they headed down the plateau into the deep valley below.

They paused when they got to the edge of the valley. "Well," said Grandpa, "what do you think? Here's a trail that's leading into the valley. Should we try it?"

"You bet," Answered the children. "We didn't come this far to turn around now."

Tied together, they cautiously entered the 'Valley of NO Return.' For the first half mile the heat was almost unbearable. Then something strange begins to happen. It started getting colder. It seemed like every step they took the temperature dropped a few degrees. By the time they reached halfway across, the wind had picked up and it was freezing.

Aria said, "Like Maddox always says, 'Jumping horny toads,' Grandpa was right. He hit the nail right on the head."

As they traveled toward the other side of the valley, the temperature dropped to 50 degrees below zero and the wind was blowing forty miles an hour. The chill factor was incredible. The frost was blowing so hard you could barely see your nose in front of your face. It was hard to see the path and they were glad they were tied together. Then the unforeseen happened, the trail forked in three different directions.

"Which way do we go now Grandpa?" asked the children.

Grandpa got a worried look on his face as he contemplated their next move. He knew that if he chose the wrong path, they could become lost in this treacherous valley and freeze to death before they could find their way out. He took out his compass, but a strange magnetic field made the needle go in all directions. It was useless.

Grandpa had the children hold hands as he prayed for guidance. He then got on his knees and studied the three trails.

"We'll take this one," said Grandpa. "It looks like it's been used more often." He took a large ball of twine out of his backpack he'd brought for just such an occasion and staked one end to the ground. "We'll unwind it as we continue," explained Grandpa, "This way we'll be able to find our way back if this trail doesn't lead anywhere.

I don't want to take any chances of getting lost." With determination and caution, he led the children deeper into the valley, unrolling the twine as he went. It wasn't long before they noticed that the temperature was getting warmer. With relief they knew they had taken the right trail that was leading them across the valley. When finally, they could faintly see the other side, the wind began to slow down and the temperature was almost back to normal.

"Wow! We would have frozen to death without these clothes." shuddered Aria. "There's no way we would have survived, especially if we'd taken the wrong trail."

"Now you can see why so many people don't make it and why it's called the 'valley of no return'," explained Grandpa.

"We sure can," said Taven. "That was the weirdest weather change I've ever seen."

When they climbed up the hill on the other side the temperature was 70 degrees. As soon as they left the death gripping cold the fog began to clear. The land was covered with high clouds and the air was warm and humid, unlike the hot, dry heat they had left on the other side.

"Look at this!" shouted Aria. "These are the largest trees I've ever seen."

"They sure are," said Grandpa. "They look like the giant sequoias of California. They must be ten feet across. It feels like we're in another part of the world instead of the far north."

The land was full of lush, green vegetation and wildflowers, unlike the cold stunted forest of the far north.

"What caused this?" asked Aria.

Grandpa scratched his head. "This is strange, very strange." Then he noticed off in the distance a row of mountains with dark, fiery red plumes rising from their peaks.

"Do you see that?" said Grandpa as he pointed to the mountains. "Those are active volcanoes. The heat coming from them must be trapped by the thick cloud cover we saw from the other side of the valley. That cold air inversion we crossed is probably what makes the constant cloud cover."

"Wow!" said Taven, "What a perfect place to live."

"And to hide from the world," said Maddox. "If the land is always covered with clouds, then no planes could ever see them. If the Bear Indians do live here, they would have it 'made in the shade', literally."

"They sure would, and they would have a year-round climate just like summer." added Grandpa. "This might be the place where the Bear Indians migrated to years ago. Let's go a little further down this trail and do some exploring."

They had hiked for several hours through lush green, jungle like foliage when suddenly Taven stopped and just stood looking up at a tree. "What in the world is that?" as he pointed up into the branches. "Something's stuck high up in this old cedar tree with feathers tied to it."

Everyone's attention turned to where he was looking.

"I'm not sure what it is," said Grandpa. "Get on my shoulders and let me boost you up to those lower branches."

Taven climbed on Grandpa's shoulder and took hold of a branch. He then scooted up the tree like a squirrel and in a flash came to the strange object.

"Will you look at this; it's a spear." He yelled down. With a heavy tug he pulled the spear out of the tree and held it out for all to see.

"Be careful coming down," cautioned Grandpa.

When he reached the ground, everyone gathered around for a closer look.

"Wow," said Aria. "Looks like an Indian spear with all those feathers tied to it."

"Jumping horny toads!" exclaimed Maddox. "There's a symbol of a bear on the other side. This has got to be from the tribe of the Bear Indians."

Grandpa agreed. "You're probably right, Maddox. This proves that the Bear Indians were here at one time. We'll do some more exploring tomorrow and see what we can find, but first we probably should stop and make camp while we've got some daylight left. We need to make plans on what to do next. I've been thinking, If the Bear Indians are here, it might be very dangerous to try and make contact with them. They, along with the cold weather, could be the reason the entrance to this place is called the 'Valley of No Return'. We need to be extra cautious."

The children agreed and began setting up their tents and making dinner. They had just finished eating when it happened. Everyone froze and looked at each other. The haunting sound of the ghost drums just like the night before, louder than they had ever heard, echoed through the forest.

"What are we going to do now?" asked Aria. All the kids looked at Grandpa with questioning eyes. Grandpa starred out into the darkness. "I'm glad we stopped when we did. It's too dangerous to be wondering around out here in the dark, especially with those Indian drums beating. In the morning we'll decide what to do. Either turn around and head back home or see if we can locate where those drums are coming from. For now, we need to get some sleep and be rested for tomorrow. We need to be extra careful and make wise decisions in the morning. Before turning in, Grandpa led them in a prayer asking God to protect and lead them in the direction they should go.

CHAPTER 5

THE LOST TRIBE

As the full moon began to rise, the 'Ceremony of the Bear' would once more be celebrated, just like it had been for generations by the tribe of the Bear Indians. They considered the grizzly bear sacred for its mighty strength and bravery. No other animal in the north woods was more respected. Four times a year the tribe would gather to honor this monarch of the north with a special offering of food. Large quantities of berries, fish and grain soaked in animal fat would be placed in wooden troughs for the bears to eat. The wooden troughs were in a deep ravine with shear rock walls located just outside of their camp. This would provide a safe viewing of the bears as the tribe would gather along the edge of the rock cliffs. When all the preparations were made, the bears would be called with the beating of the drums. Over the years, every bear in the territory had learned that the sound of those drums meant abundant food and would literally run towards the rock walled canyon whenever they heard it. They had become so accustomed to this feast that they acted more like tame bears than wild ones. They didn't come to fight each other but just to get their fill of the plentiful food the Indians provided.

This year the ceremony was a very special one. It included what was called, the 'passage of manhood and would last two days.' Whenever an Indian boy turned 14 years old, he could choose to become part of this ritual. This year there would be four candidates and Watonga, the Chief's son would be one of them. Running Bear, the Chief, was very anxious in his heart as he knew this ritual was dangerous and could cost his only son, Watonga, his life. Every boy that succeeded would no longer be considered a child but a worthy brave of the tribe. Sadly, not everyone passed this test.

The passage of manhood went like this. At the 'Ceremony of the Bears' the young boys who had turned 14 would watch the bears gather down in the rock canyon feasting on the abundance of food. From this safe vantage point, each boy would choose a bear. The larger the bear, the greater the honor would be if he was successful. After the bears finished their meal and headed back into the woods, the boys would follow their chosen bear with the challenge of passing the test of manhood. They were not allowed to take a spear, bow or even a knife for protection. The bears were never to be harmed or they would fail the test. The objective was to get close enough to dab a color of dye on the bear's fur. Each boy was given a leather pouch of white paint made from limestone to mark his bear. The next evening, the bears would be called back once more for a feast by the beating of the drums. The tribal council would examine the bears and the boy whose paint was on his bear would be promoted to manhood. As you would expect, this was very, very dangerous. The best chance of success was to wait until the bear fell asleep and then try to slip up on him as quiet as a mouse. Only an Indian boy could approach a sleeping bear and mark it with paint without waking it up. Even so, some have failed this test. Some were mauled and maimed for life and some went to what's called the 'happy hunting grounds.'

Watonga and the three other boys gathered on the edge of the rock cliffs where they could watch the bears when they came to feed. The food had been placed in the troughs and the drums began to beat. Boom,.....boom boom boom, Boom,.....boom boom boom. After about twenty minutes the first bear arrived. It was a small cub about the size of a dog. The boys laughed. "There you go Watonga," joked one of the boys. "He doesn't look too ferocious."

"Oh yeah," said Watonga, "what about its mother." Coming out of the forest behind the cub was a huge mama bear making sure her little cub was safe. "It would be easier to paint her than her baby," said Watonga. The boys didn't speak another word as bears began pouring out of the woods. They knew the chief's son should have the first pick.

"Which one do you want?" they asked. "You should pick the biggest bear for the most honor."

"No," said Watonga, "We'll draw straws for the order of choosing. That way it will be fair for everyone." The straws were cut in different lengths with the longest straw going first to the shortest being last to choose his bear. Of the four boys, it was Watonga that got the shortest straw. The others carefully chose their bear, picking the largest three in the group. When it became Watonga's turn, there were only average size bears left to choose from. A feeling of disappointment came over him as he was about to pick a smaller bear than his friends had picked. Then something happened that the Bear Indians hadn't seen in many years. The ground shook as a huge bear came into the clearing. Its roar was deafening and when it stood up on its hind legs, it was taller than three bears put together. The other bears gave it plenty of room as it walked towards the feed troughs. Watonga knew this was the bear he must choose. Part of him was happy because of the honor this bear would bring him but deep inside he was fearful of trying to mark such a monster bear.

Just as he was about to choose, his father put his hand on his shoulder. "Son," said the chief, "You don't have to choose this gigantic bear. It would be very dangerous." The chief had a worried look on his face as any father would have for his son, but he knew the choice was not up to him.

"Father, I chose this one," said Watonga "It will be alright. The great spirit will protect me."

Just then, the giant bear raised up on his hind legs and raised his paws high in the air. His right paw had only one claw on it. The tribe starred in disbelief and then began shouting in unison.

"Single Claw! Single Claw!"

"He's come back again," thundered the Chief. "The great spirit bear Single Claw has returned to honor our village like he did at our last celebration." The legend of Single Claw had been told for many years around the campfires of the Bear Indians. They had great respect for this gigantic bear. It wasn't often that this monarch of the north ventured across the 'Valley of No Return,' into the land called the Barrens.

Watonga secretly wished in his heart that he had not chosen this gigantic bear, but once a choice was made it could not be taken back.

Later that night after the bears had eaten their fill, they ambered back into the woods. The four boys seeking manhood knew this would be the best time to try to catch them sleeping and paint their mark on them. After eating such a large meal, the bears would be looking for a place to rest.

Each boy was handed a leather pouch of paint and a long stick with a rag tied to the end. This would be their paint brush to mark their bear. Showing much bravery, they headed out into the moonlit night, knowing full well they might never return.

CHAPTER 6

THE DEADLY TEST

Watonga kept going over in his mind the things his father and the tribal elders had taught him about bears. He knew he must obey every law of the forest if he was going to survive this test of manhood. The danger of waking a sleeping bear while painting a spot on him could cost him his life. Every Indian knew that when traveling through the forest you should make lots of noise. You always carried a few stones that rattled inside a birch bark box to let the bears know you were coming down the trail. This way, they weren't startled and had time to get out of the way, which they almost always did. But if you surprised them, you had a much greater chance of being mauled. This is why the test of manhood was so dangerous. You never, ever wanted to startle or surprise a bear but now the boys must quietly sneak up on them without letting them know they're coming.

It was easy to follow the bear's tracks because of the full moon and in the far north it stays light most of the night. Single Claw's tracks were especially easy to follow because he made such deep imprints in the soft dirt. For several miles Watonga followed them before they vanished into a dark, scary looking cave in the side of a mountain. His heart began to pound as he knew this would be the place he must enter if he was ever to become a warrior of his tribe. The cave was large and very dark, making it was almost impossible to see anything. He would give the bear time to fall asleep before attempting to paint the white spot on its fur. The problem would be guessing when he was asleep. When do bears go to sleep anyway, Running Bear pondered. He stopped at the entrance of the cave and listened. He could hear Single Claw breathing at the back of the cave. Indian boys have tremendous senses of hearing and smell. It wasn't long before the breathing became slower and softer, indicating the bear was probably sleeping. This was the best time to try and mark this gigantic bear. He must paint his bear now or lose his chance of manhood in the tribe for another year. To wait this long for a second chance would be a disgrace for a Chief's son. Slowly, Watonga inched his way deeper into the dark, damp cave. He could smell the strong odor of the bear as he entered. There was barely enough moonlight to see his hand in front of his face. His heart was pounding so hard he thought surely the bear would hear it. Closer and closer he came. He was now so close he could smell the bear's breath. Slowly he moved closer and closer to his prize for manhood. After about half an hour of slow creeping, he figured he was within range. He carefully reached into his pouch for his birch bark box of paint. Dipping his cloth covered stick into the paint he extended it toward the bear's side. This is where he must be very, very careful. Too hard and the bear would awaken. Too soft and the mark wouldn't show, and all his effort would be for nothing. He placed the rag on the bear. Everything seemed fine and then the bear woofed and turned. Watonga froze, waiting to see if he had woken this sleeping monster. The few seconds seemed like an eternity. He gently pulled the stick back and laid it by his side. Finally, the bear let out a deep breath and rolled back over for more sleep. A sigh of relief came over the fearful boy. He had done it! His bear was marked! All he had to do now was quietly slip out of the cave. Moving backwards where you couldn't see his feet was much more difficult. Coming to the mouth of the cave, he had only inches to go when his foot bumped against a loose rock. It rolled down and bumped into another rock with a loud crack. Single Claws' eyes popped open in full alert peering into the darkness to see what had caused the noise. His eyes starred directly into the eyes of a freighted Indian boy. A deafening roar filled the cave. Running Bear knew he had only a fraction of a second to try and get away. With lightning speed, he sprung out of the cave just as Single Claw swung his massive claw, making a clean slice in his leather vest. With agility and speed driven by adrenaline, he jumped out of the cave into a tall Cedar tree next to the entrance. Reaching for branches he scrambled higher and higher as fast as he could. The bear was right behind him. With another roar Single Claw jumped and swung at his intruder. The wind from his paw was felt on Running Bear's face but he never slowed down. He kept climbing higher to safety with the speed of a squirrel. He knew that large bears can't climb trees. They're too heavy to hoist themselves up on the branches and if they could the branches would easily break. Watonga breathed a sigh of relief knowing that he was safe. At least for the time being. Never in his life had he been so scared. When his heart finally stopped pounding, he looked down at the largest bear he had ever seen. Single Claw was pacing around the tree. He would stop and look up, then let out a deafening roar that could be heard for miles. Running Bear wondered how long that bear would keep him trapped high up in the branches.

CHAPTER 7

TRAPPED

When our rested explorers woke the next morning, there was excitement in the air for they knew they were getting close to solving the mystery of the Bear Indians.

"Grandpa," asked Aria, "Are we going to follow the sound of the drums we heard last night or head back home."

Grandpa, rubbing his chin, pondered the decision. "Well, I've been thinking all night. Perhaps we should go just a little ways farther since we've come this far. We'll head toward the volcanoes. That's the direction the drums seemed to come from. If we don't find something by noon, we'll turn around and head home. We sure don't want to get lost in this land of giant trees, my compass still isn't working for some reason."

"Sounds good to me," said Aria. "This place kind of gives me the creeps."

"Yeah, me too," chimed in Taven and Maddox.

It wasn't long before they had broke camp and were heading off in the direction they had heard the drums last night. They hadn't gone far when Maddox stopped. "Quiet everyone, I think I hear something."

"What?" said Taven. "Those horny toads you keep talking about?"

"No Silly, just listen."

A few minutes went by, and they were just about to move on when they all heard it.

"There," said Maddox. "Did you hear it?"

They all nodded their heads. Grandpa got a worried look on his face.

"That was the roar of a bear. A large bear."

Aria was the first to figure it out. "I think I know why you look worried Grandpa. That sounds like Single Claw, doesn't it?"

Grandpa slowly nodded his head.

They had heard that roar many times before and knew there was only one bear that sounded like that, Single Claw. His roar was deep and loud and would send chills down your spine.

"What would Single Claw be doing over here in the barrens?" asked Taven.

"I don't know," answered Grandpa, "But it sure sounds like him. If he wanted to cross through the Valley of No Return, he could do so in a matter of minutes. With his speed and thick fur coat, the freezing cold would have no effect on him."

"Maybe it has something to do with those drums we keep hearing." asked Maddox.

"Could be," said Grandpa. "I think it would be wise to get your weapons out of your packs, just in case we run into trouble. After all, the scripture says 'prepare your minds for action.'

That didn't bother the kids in the slightest since they loved every excuse to carry their spear, knives, bow and arrows, and sword and shield that they were extremely efficient with. The many hours of practice gave them a skill that soon would prove invaluable.

Grandpa asked if they wanted to keep going or turn back.

"Turn back!" They all questioned. "Why, we've come this far and there's no way we want to quit now." said Maddox.

"Yeah," agreed Aria. "Besides, every time we've heard Single Claw roar like that it means he's seen a campfire or got someone trapped that he's trying to get to. I think we need to continue just in case someone might be in some real trouble."

"That's all I needed to know, and I agree," said Grandpa. He began clearing a trail with his machete toward the direction of the roaring bear. The underbrush was thick and slowed their progress until they came across a well-worn trail along a riverbank. It was much easier, and they began making good progress. The roar of the bear became louder with every mile they covered telling them they were going in the right direction. What they didn't know was, Running Bear, the chief of the Bear Indians was also following the sound of that raging bear along with a dozen of his warriors looking for his son.

Watonga was the only one of the four boys that didn't come back to the village the night before to complete his test of manhood. One of the boys had a close call as his bear took a swipe at him. His injuries were slight, and he would heal with a story of bravery. The frequent roar of a bear coming from deep in the forest was the only clue as to what might have happened to the Chiefs son.

CHAPTER 8

IMPOSSIBLE RESCUE

Watonga clung to the branches high above the ground as he watched the largest bear in the world, Single Claw, pace around the tree letting out a blood curdling roar every few minutes. He had been doing this all night with no sign of quitting. The young Indian boy was beginning to tire of holding on and wondered how much longer he could keep this up. If he dozed off, he could easily fall to his death. He took off his vest and used it to tie his arm around a small branch. This way, if he did fall asleep, he wouldn't tumble into the arms of that killer bear. How long could he go without food and water? Will anyone come to his rescue? And even if they did, how could they fight such a gigantic bear? He was becoming discouraged when Single Claw stopped circling the tree and went back inside the cave. Maybe this is my chance, he thought. After waiting about an hour, with Single Claw still inside the cave, Watonga began descending down the tall tree. Slowing and quietly he lowered himself from branch to branch. Finally getting low enough so he could peer inside the cave. It was dark inside and he couldn't see any sign of the bear. He was just a few feet above the ground and about to jump down when light reflected from two large eyes staring directly at him. It was Single Claw! It was a trap! Instantly he started back up the tree. The bear charged from the cave with lighting speed, missing his prey only by inches. Once again the speed of a strong, young Indian boy had saved him from certain death. Back up to the top he flew from the claws of death. "I must be more careful," he scolded himself. "That bear is smarter than I thought. How will I ever get back to my people?"

It wasn't long before Chief Running Bear and twelve of his braves came out onto a high clearing where they could see the bear that was making all the uproar far below. They crouched down and crawled closer to find out why he was so angry. Running Bear motioned for them to be quiet. The bear was circling a large cedar tree and would often look up into the branches. "Why is he doing this they thought. He must have something trapped up in that tree." Then one of the braves saw movement high up in the top branches. Using hand signals, he communicated to Chief Running Bear to watch the top of the tree. After A few minutes Running Bear also saw some movement. What could it be? A few minutes passed before the mystery object moved a branch out of his way. Chief Running Bear gasped. "It's, Watonga! He whispered to the braves. He's alive!"

Relief and Joy filled Running Bear's heart knowing that his son had not been killed. Now he must rescue him. But how? Never had he fought a bear as large and as strong as Single Claw. Chief Running Bear had a worried, determined look on his face. He knew what he had to do.

"You braves pay close attention to my plan. Follow me as I go down the mountain. You are to wait, out of sight, at the valley floor. I will try to draw that bear away from Running Bear. When he charges me, you are to run and get Watonga out of the tree. Take him back to the village as quick as you can. He will be your new chief. The braves were startled at what their chief was telling them.

"But Chief, you will be killed! There must be another way. Don't end your life this way."

"Show me then and I will listen, but you know there is no other way. I will lay down my life for my son. He is young and has many years left. I am old and have seen many moons. It won't be long before I go to the great spirit anyway. This is what must happen."

Sadly, they agreed to his plan. Chief Running Bear and his Braves started to make their way down the mountain to that killer bear. The hearts of the Indians were heavy with grief at the thought of losing their chief. Running Bear began his decent to death.

———————)❮⟨❍⟩❯(❮———————

Grandpa and his three grandchildren had been following the roar of an obviously angry bear most of the day. Progress was slow as they traveled through an overgrown trail just above a small river. They knew they were getting close as the roaring got louder and louder. Tension was in the air and everyone was on high alert.

"Grandpa," whispered Taven. "We must be getting close. Sounds like that bear is right around the next bend. What are we going to do?"

"We've going to see why that bear's so mad before we make any plans." Grandpa knew this was very dangerous and knew they must be extra cautious.

When they rounded the next bend of the trail, Grandpa was the first to see the bear. He held out his hand and motioned for everyone to be real quiet.

"Drop down and hide behind these bushes before the bear see's us." Grandpa whispered. "There he is, look, just under that large tree about a hundred yards away. He's standing in front of a cave against the hillside.

"And he sure looks like Single Claw!" said Aria, peering out from her cover. The way he keeps circling and looking up tells us he's got something treed up there in those branches."

"Jumping horny toads," whispered Maddox. "I see it. It's a boy holding on for dear life at the top of the tree."

"What will we do now Grandpa," asked Aria. "Do you think it's really Single Claw!"

"If I'm not mistaken," Grandpa surmised, "That bear is Single Claw! There's only one bear in the world I know with the size and roar like he has."

"You're right," said Taven. "That's got to be Single Claw."

"Remember the oath we took when we became the Bear Hunters?" reminded Grandpa. "To help those in danger from that killer bear. Well, here's an opportunity to fulfill that vow. Hears what I think we should do."

The children listened intently as Grandpa laid out a plan.

"We've fought this bear before and we know his ways. We're not afraid of him and he knows it. That's to our advantage also. Now what's the one thing we've used many times to distract and gain the upper hand on this giant bear?

"Why, it's fire." answered William. "Almost every time we've been able to draw him away by starting a fire."

"That's right," agreed Grandpa. "We all know how much he hates fire after being burned years ago and how he chases it to put it out instead of running from it. So, we're going to try it one more time."

"But Grandpa," asked Aria, "What if he's getting used to that trick? Do you think he's wise to us by now?"

"Maybe, but that's our best course of action, we'll have to take that chance." answered Grandpa. "If that fails then it's hand to hand combat and we've won that one before."

After a quick prayer, asking God to protect and guide them, they took up their positions as Grandpa had instructed them.

Running Bear stepped out into the clearing wearing his chief's head dress. Standing still for a moment, knowing this would be his last day on earth. He was just about to draw the bear's attention when something happened that caught him by surprise.

A young girl also stepped out into the open about 100 feet to his left. Aria was holding her bow loaded with a flaming arrow. When the bear saw them, he turned and let out a deafening roar, raising up on his hind legs, pawing the air. Running Bear was puzzled to see she showed no fear as she stood there facing Single Claw. He was sure she would be torn to pieces. His mind was racing. Who is she? Where did she come from? Am I having a dream? Before he could clear his mind, she pulled back and let the arrow fly right over the bear's head. What looked like a miss was really a perfect shot. The arrow flew straight and true to its target, inside the cave's entrance where it lit the dry leaves and twigs laying on the cave floor. It was then that she noticed the Indian standing to her right. She didn't have time to react as Single Claw turned and roared into the cave, thrashing and clawing at the fire she had started.

Grandpa hollered, "Quick, get the boy down." as they all ran out to help. They knew they only had a few minutes before Single Claw could put out the fire and come after them.

Chief Running Bear was still confused at what he was seeing, it was happening so quickly. When he realized, these people were trying to save his son he motioned to his Braves to come and help them. It wasn't clear who was the most surprised, the 'Bear Hunters' or the Indians but they all realized they had the same goal, saving the boy trapped at the top of the tree.

Watonga looked down from his perch high up in the tree at all the people. They were waving for him to climb down, keeping silent so as not to attract the bear who was still fighting the fire inside the cave. Seeing his father, he shot down the tree like a falling rock. Running Bear hugged his son and quickly ordered his braves to head back to the village. He turned and looked at Grandpa and his Grandchildren, who had been watching with amazement at what was happening and motioned for them to follow him also. The Indians led the retreat, scrambling up the steep mountain trail. The Bear Hunters were just about to leave the clearing and start up the trail, just behind the Indians, when it happened! A roar from outside the cave. Single Claw had extinguished the fire and was coming after them. Running Bear ordered his Braves to keep going and get his son back to the safety of the village. When he turned around, he couldn't believe what he was seeing. The Bear Hunters were going back to fight that bear! Never had he seen braver warriors than this. Who were they anyway? He had to stay and help.

CHAPTER 9

FIGHT FOR LIFE

The bear hunters moved quickly back into the clearing to make their stand. Aria with her bow and arrow, Tavin with his sword and shield and Maddox with his spear and throwing knives. Grandpa had an old lever action Winchester rifle. Their goal was never to kill this magnificent creature but to stop his charge on the retreating Indians and drive him back into the woods.

Chief Running Bear watched as the children quickly formed a line of defense. Grandpa slowed the bear's charge by firing a couple of shots into the air. This gave the bear hunters time to encircle Single Claw. The bear was confused as his attackers were now on all sides. Before he could decide who to go after first, Aria drew back her bow a fired an arrow right into Single Claws bottom. With a roar, he quickly spun around, swatting the arrow away from him as it felt like a bee sting. In fact, that's all the damage it would do since Single Claw's hide was as thick and tough as a board. Even Grandpa's gun wouldn't penetrate this bear's hide. Their goal was to distract him long enough that he'd get frustrated and give up the fight. Tavin ran up with his sword and shield and poked the bear's foot. Another roar came as Single Claw spun around and slapped Tavin's shield send him flying in the air but unhurt. Now it was Maddox's turn. He launched two throwing knives into the bears hide that infuriated and frustrated this creature who was used to his opponents running with fear at his tremendous size and roar, not standing to fight. He kept spinning around as the bear hunters continued their merry go round style of attack. Grandpa would occasionally fire his gun over the bear's head to further confuse him. Chief Running Bear watched at a distance as their choreographed attack kept this monster bear at bay. This is what they had practiced over and over, and it had worked successfully in the past. Single Claw would soon tire of this constant barrage and go charging back into the woods. At least, that's what he was supposed to do.

The bear hunters noticed that this time Single Claw wasn't responding to their plan of attack like he'd done in the past. He didn't seem to be getting tired of their little bee stings. What was happening though, they were starting to get tired. Exhaustion was beginning to set in. Over and over, they were inflicting their weapons on him, and he wasn't running off. Grandpa saw what was happening and knew he had to do something. He aimed his rifle over the bear's head to fire another shot. When he squeezed the trigger, nothing happened. His gun had jammed.

"Quick," he shouted. "Break your positions and head for the cave! We must hold him off there. Keep facing forward with your weapons and back into the cave."

Chief Running Bear saw what was happening and joined their retreat. After they entered the cave, they set up their defensive positions. They knew this might be their final battle with Single Claw. He seemed to have more endurance than ever while they were feeling fatigue from their tired muscles.

The bear made a gallant charge but was held back by the brave bear hunters one more time.

"Grandpa, how long can we hold him off?" pleaded Aria. "We're running out of strength!"

Tavin and Maddox shook their heads in agreement. Grandpa had never seen Single Claw act this way. He usually would run off after a few minutes of battle. But this was not to be.

In all the excitement, they hadn't noticed Chief Running Bear who had run inside the cave with them. He sensed their dismay as they waited for the next attack. Grandpa told the children to bow their heads. As he began to pray, Running Bear knew that this old man was asking the Great Spirit to help them. Running Bear bowed his head too.

"Some trust in chariots and some in horses, but we trust in the name of the Lord our God. We ask you to deliver us from this danger and we do trust in you. In Jesus name we pray, amen."

It was a quick prayer as Single Claw was preparing another charge. The huge creature was swaying back and forth in front of the cave, starring directly at them.

Even through all of this, the children showed no fear.

That's when Single Claw did something that totally baffled them. He laid down at the cave's entrance, trapping his victims inside. He knew they couldn't get out and he would just out last them.

"What in the world is he doing?" asked Tavin. "He's just lying there as if he's tired."

"He's not tired," answered Grandpa. "He knows he's got us trapped and he'll just wait until we have to come out for food and water. That's a very smart bear."

They were all desperately in need of water from the battle and glad they had a reprieve for rest.

Suddenly Chief Running Bear got excited about something he saw and began to speak for the first time.

"look, Look! He shouted.

He pointed to Single Claw who was rolled over on his side.

Everyone strained their eyes to see what he was looking at.

"I don't see anything," said Aria.

"Me neither," responded the others.

Running Bear pointed and with a loud voice, "White paint! See the white mark on his underside!"

They were all surprised to hear him speak and curious about his excitement over a white spot, on Single Claws belly.

"What does that mean?" asked Grandpa.

"It's why my son, Watonga, was here. He has passed his test of manhood." explained the Chief.

Everyone was confused about what the Chief was telling them.

Running Bear was about to explain more when Single Claw rose and stood on his hind legs. He let out a roar that thundered in the forest.

"Back to you positions!" shouted Grandpa. "Looks like he changed his mind about waiting us out and is getting ready for another attack."

Everyone grabbed their weapons knowing their chances were very slim. Single Claw was more determined than ever to finally finish off the bear hunters that had defeated him so many times before.

"Don't give up." encouraged Grandpa. "It's not over till it's over. God can find a way when it seems impossible. Hold your ground and don't give up."

The children nodded their heads in agreement knowing it would take a miracle to get them out of this one.

The angry bear started for the cave when a distant noise caused him to stop in mid stride. He cocked his head and peered toward the direction the sound was coming from.

"Look," said Aria. "He stopped! Looks like he hears something."

"Listen! Don't you hear it?" exclaimed Grandpa. "It's drums!"

The faint sound of drums grew louder and louder.

"Jumping horny toads, It's the ghost drums!" shouted Maddox.

Chief Running Bear smiled. "Those aren't ghost drums. They are the drums from my village. We play them for the 'Ceremony of the Bear.' Tonight is the second night we honor the grizzly and is the night our young boys become braves as they pass the test of manhood."

The chief quickly explained what the ceremony was about and why the drums were being played.

"The bears have learned that the sound of those drums means a great feast. They come to gorge themselves on the abundant food my people have prepared for them. This helps them store fat for their winter hibernation."

"So that's why He had so much energy." reasoned Grandpa.

It was then the miracle happened. Single Claw turned from his deadly attack and exploded into the forest, following the sound of the ghost drums.

CHAPTER 10

THE LOST TRIBE

C hief Running Bear dashed out of the cave. He looked back and motioned to his companions.

"Hurry, we must move now! Follow me. I will take you to my village."

They needed no encouragement as they quickly left the confines of the dark cave.

He led them up the trail to the top of the ridge. The others were amazed at the speed and endurance he possessed. For an older man he moved like a deer through the forest. It was all grandpa could do to keep up. The children were panting too and glad when he finally stopped. He signaled with his hand, peering into the forest as if hearing something. Suddenly, dozens of armed warriors lunged out of the woods and surrounded them. All the able-bodied warriors of the village had headed back for their chief after Running Bear was safely brought into camp.

"Chief Running Bear," they shouted. "You're alive! Did that bear injure you?"

Running Bear turned to Grandpa and his Grandchildren.

"No, I'm unhurt, thanks to these brave people. They fought off Single Claw and saved my life."

"Who are these white warriors and where did they come from?" Asked one of the braves.

"They'll be time for that later. First, we must get back to our village before the passage of manhood is over." instructed Chief Running Bear. The drums could still be heard echoing through the forest.

As they hurried back to the 'ceremony of the bear,' Grandpa and the bear hunters were bewildered as to what was happening. Questions where whirling in their mind. Is this the lost tribe of the Bear Indians? What is the passage of manhood and the ceremony of the bear? Why are those drums beating and why do the bears run toward them?

And curiously, why do they all speak English?

As they got close to the village, they followed a trail that brought them to a rock cliff overlooking a deep canyon. They starred in amazement at the scene below them. Down on the canyon floor, dozens of bears, more bears than they had ever seen in one place before, were feeding on piles of food placed in wooden troughs. A full moon, casting a golden glow through the cloud cover, added to this mysterious scene. A tribal elder sitting beside their counsel fire was beating on a huge leather drum. It's constant BOOM, boom boom boom, Boom, boom, boom, boom resonated for miles around. Every few minutes, a new bear would come running out of the forest and join the feast.

The Chief saw the questioning faces on Grandpa and the bear hunters. He began to explain to them what they were witnessing. The ceremony of the bear, the passage of manhood by marking the bears with paint, the beating of the drums to call the bears to their feast. He told them that this was the second night of their ceremony when the tribal elders would look for the painted bears to return, initiating the boys as brave warriors to the tribe.

It was all beginning to make sense when Tavin asked. "Excuse me, Mr. Chief, there's one thing we'd like to know. What is the name of your tribe? Are you called the Bear Indians?

The chief smiled. "You are right. We are called the Bear Indians."

It was the question on everyone's mind and glad that Tavin had asked. It confirmed their suspicions.

"Now it's my turn." began Running Bear. "I also have many questions about you. Who are you? Where did you come from? Why do you call yourselves 'the bear hunters'? Why did you come here to our land?

Before Grandpa could answer a commotion arose from the tribe. They had spotted the first bear with a white mark painted on it.

"Look, a 'manhood bear'!" Shouted one of the tribal elders.

"That one's mine!" claimed one of the boys beaming with pride.

It wasn't long before two more painted bears were spotted. Three boys had just become official braves of the tribe. The only one left was Watonga, the chief's son.

Where was Single Claw? He should have been here by now. Watonga was anxious that all the danger he experienced could be for nothing. How shameful it would be if the only one not to make it to manhood was the Chief's son.

"Father, you told me you saw the white spot on Single Claw, didn't you? Asked Watonga.

"Yes, son. But the law of the tribe says the tribal elders must be the ones to witness it. There is nothing I can do."

"But Chief, we saw it too." said Aria, "Doesn't that count for something?"

"I wish it did, but it doesn't." answered Running Bear with a discouraged face. They waited several more hours before Running Bear held his spear over his head and announced to his people, "It's time to let the fires die out and head back to the village." He turned to Watonga and said, "Maybe next year, my son, you will be successful."

With heavy hearts Chief Running Bear and the tribe started back to the village. The elders had just left when it happened. A roar that shook the trees! Everyone froze in their tracks.

"Jumping horny toads. It's him!" exclaimed Maddow. "It's Single Claw."

They all turned and raced back to the rock ledge.

"Look father, It's Single Claw. He finally came!" Watonga yelled with excitement and relief as he watched this huge bear enter the clearing down below.

The elders looked for the white spot but couldn't see it. Chief Running bear told them it was there. "It was under his back legs.

Keep looking!" he said. "I know it's there."

Even though they believed the chief, by counsel law, they had to witness it themselves too to make it official. Just when it seemed hopeless, they heard another ear-splitting roar. The largest bear in the world stood up on his hind legs, pawing the air, as if to say, 'I am king!' It was then that a white spot on his underside could be seen. The whole tribe cheered with shouts and war hoops when they spotted the last 'man hood' bear. Watonga let out a sigh of relief. Now he would be considered a man, a Brave of the Bear Indians. A very courageous Brave at that because of Single Claw's size. This would earn him the coveted Eagle Feather for marking the largest bear.

The chief turned to Grandpa and his Grand kids. "Tomorrow, I want to introduce you to my village, but before I do, we must finish our talk. In the morning you can explain everything about yourselves. Right now, we must return to my village and get some rest.

This was good news as they were all exhausted from the day's events.

When they arrived at the village they were amazed at the size and order of the lodges.

"Wow!" said Aria, "I was expecting teepee's. "They have small, wooden lodges with cedar shake roofs."

The buildings were laid out in an orderly fashion like a small western town. At the end of their village was a much larger structure with massive log poles for its entrance. That is where the Chief lives. Running Bear led them to his lodge and gave them caribou skins to sleep on. There's nothing warmer and softer than caribou fur. The only light was from a small dim, 'rush candle' dipped in animal fat in the center of the room. The darkness hid the worried, concerned expression on Grandpa's face.

"Rest well my white warriors. Tomorrow you will meet my people." comforted Running Bear as he entered his sleeping chamber.

Sleep came fast after the action-packed day they had just experienced.

CHAPTER 11

ESCAPE

"Wake up, you sleepy heads!" called Grandpa. "Chief Running Bear has been up for hours and already lit his morning fires. He's fixing breakfast for us over at the ceremony lodge."

"I still can't believe it." said Tavin. Rubbing the sleep from his eyes. "Here we are at the lost tribe of the Bear Indians."

"I know," agreed Maddox. "And sleeping in the Chief's lodge. Who would believe it."

Aria nodded her head and asked Grandpa. "When are we going to head back home? I bet Grandma is starting to get worried."

Grandpa didn't answer for a moment and then said, "Get a move on. They'll be waiting for us."

When they entered the ceremony lodge, they were surprised that Chief Running Bear was by himself fixing breakfast for them.

"Good morning, Chief," greeted Grandpa. "We were expecting more members of your tribe."

"That will come later," explained Running Bear. "Like I said yesterday, first we must finish our talk."

After breakfast, Grandpa explained to the chief who they were. That they were from the town of Sawdust Springs on the south side of Bear Mountain. He explained all about Single Claw and how they had rescued many people from his anger over campfires. That's why they were called the 'Bear Hunters."

The chief listened intently when Grandpa told the story about Cactus Calhoon and how he was saved by the ghost drums while prospecting on the Caribou River. How their friend, Rawhide Jake had heard the drums several times when the north wind blew down the river from the valley of no return.

"Ghost drums?" The chief smiled. "We never thought the drums would carry as far as Bear Mountain. It must have been the north wind. We must only beat them from now on when a south wind blows. I will tell my tribe about this important finding."

"We were only looking for an answer about the ghost drums." explained Grandpa. "That's why we came here in the first place. It was a mystery to us since we don't really believe in ghost."

"I'm glad you did." said Running Bear. "You saved my son's life, and also mine. Because of your bravery you will be given a lodge of you own and welcomed into our tribe."

"Are you kidding?" asked Aria. "We will be honorary members of your tribe?"

"Not just honorary members, but full members of the tribe." answered Running Bear.

The children didn't understand Grandpa's next question. "Does this have anything to do with the valley of no return?" he asked with a serious look.

Chief Running Bear paused before he answered. With sadness in his eyes, he said, "Yes it does. Since we came to this land over a hundred years ago, escaping a dreaded cholera epidemic, we made a law that if anyone could cross the valley of no return and live through it, they would not be allowed to leave. You are the first to do so. We must keep our presence here a secret. We are afraid that if people discovered this land of fire and warmth, we would be driven from it. That is why you must not be allowed to leave."

The children listened in shock at what they had just heard.

"What!" exclaimed Aria. "You mean we are prisoners here? What about our friends, our family, our school, our horses. We can't stay here! Our whole life is back at Sawdust Springs."

"I'm sorry." said the chief. "You won't be prisoners; you will be treated like royalty."

"We don't want to be treated like royalty!" shouted Taven. "We want to go home!"

"I understand." consoled the chief. "It is out of my hands. It is our sacred law."

Grandpa told the chief they needed time to themselves to digest this turn of events.

"We would like to go back to your lodge and pray about this. Our God will be with us."

Chief Running Bear agreed but placed armed warriors around the lodge in case they tried to escape.

As the shocked children gathered inside the dim lit lodge, Grandpa gathered them around him.

"We must ask God for help. Let's Pray."

"The psalmist said, 'God is our refuge and strength, therefore we will not fear."

Grandpa encouraged them to 'Trust in the Lord with all their heart and lean not on their own understanding. In all their ways to acknowledge God and He will direct their paths.'

Aria said, "But Grandpa, how in the world could we get out of here since we are guarded by so many Indians?"

"Yeah," said Taven. "And we are trapped on this side of that freezing valley with no warm clothes to cross back through it."

"And no one knows where we are!" chimed in Maddox.

"Children, that's where faith comes in. Can't you see that you are putting God in a box and limiting Him by your lack of faith. Don't you realize that He can do anything!"

Grandpa went on to explain that if God wants to do something, nothing can stop Him. And that includes rescuing them. All we need to do is have enough faith to trust Him and obey His commands.

"I know you're right," said Aria. "We're tired and this just hit us like a ton of bricks."

"I had my suspicions about this but didn't want say anything and worry you," said Grandpa. "But one thing I will tell you, in my heart I have a peace that we will make it back to Sawdust Springs. I don't know how but God does."

Grandpa's faith was a great encouragement to all his grandchildren.

Later that day, Chief Running Bear introduced the 'white warriors,' as he called them, to his village. He told the tribe how they had saved his life and also Watonga's. The tribe was grateful and honored to have them as members. They said if there was anything they needed, just ask. They treated their new captives with much respect.

But the 'white warriors' had only one thing on their mind....... ESCAPE!

The next day, Chief Running Bear looked in on his rescuers to see how they were doing.

"We're doing O K," answered Grandpa. "But we have one request. Would you have a council meeting to see if the law could be changed to let us go home?"

The chief looked doubtful. "I don't think it will do any good but because you saved my son's life, I'll try."

This gave the children a little hope anyway. Grandpa paused for a moment and then said, "There's one other thing I've been wanting to ask you. Why do you and your people speak English instead of your native tongue? How did you learn it?"

Chief Running Bear smiled. "It was your missionaries that taught us many moons ago. Back when our forefathers lived in the shadow of Bear Mountain. We spoke the white man's language for so long that our elders decided to continue when we moved to the Barrens."

"Just curious," said Grandpa. "That explains it."

It was hard to wait for the answer of the council members. Everywhere the captives went they were watched by guards to ensure they wouldn't try to escape. Finally, after several days of anxious waiting, Chief Running Bear lit the counsel fire and gathered the elders. He told them of his request about changing the law. After much talk, they gave their answer.

"Grandpa, look! Here comes Running Bear to tell us how the council meeting went," Shouted a hopeful Aria as the Chief headed toward his lodge where they were waiting. They were watching his expression for any clues of hope, but the chief kept a stoic look that told them nothing. He motioned for them to sit on the ground and then he began to talk.

"My friends, I'm afraid my suspicions were right. The elders won't change the law. You must remain with us. I tried to get them to change one thing though. I said, since no one can cross the valley of no return without 'warm, winter clothes', he paused and winked at Grandpa, you shouldn't have to be guarded anymore. The valley will keep you with us. But they did not agree. They said maybe in time this could happen but for now it would be better to keep an eye on you."

Grandpa and the children were disappointed but not really surprised at the verdict. They were expecting as much. After the meeting with the Chief was over, Grandpa picked up a water bucket and motioned for the children to follow him. He led them down to the creek that ran just below the village. When sure that no one could hear him, he quietly spoke. "That's it. We now have a chance to get out of here! Chief Running Bear just gave us the clue to escape. Did you see him wink when he mentioned warm winter clothes?"

"What clue?" asked Tavin. "Aren't we still trapped? We don't have our warm clothes to cross back through that frozen valley."

"I get it." said Aria. "Chief Running Bear is going to give us a chance to get out of here because of what we did for him. He knows we must have proper clothing stashed somewhere or we wouldn't have been able cross in the first place."

"That's right Aria. The chief is grateful to us for saving him and his son."

"I know he's grateful for us helping him." interrupted Maddox, "but how are we ever going to find our warm winter clothes we left back at our camp with everyone watching us? We're lost in this land!"

"Don't you see." explained Grandpa. "Our parkas are still where we left them. All we have to do is figure out a way to find them. It's a long shot since our compass doesn't work in this volcanic, magnetic land and I know we're lost, but there's still hope of a chance."

Just then one of the Indian guards came down the trail. "What are you doing here?" he commanded. "You should be back at your lodge."

"Isn't this the best place to get water?" answered Grandpa. Hoping their conversation hadn't been overheard.

The guard thought for a moment and then nodded his head. "Hear, let me help carry the water bucket."

They all breathed a sigh of relief.

When they returned to the Chief's lodge, Running Bear was there waiting for them.

"I'm going to move you to my other private lodge so you will have a little more privacy. This is a special lodge my grandfather built years ago at the edge of the village and you will have it all to yourselves."

They were appreciative of the Chiefs efforts but were only interested in one thing. Finding their parkas so they could get back home.

The next day passed slowly as they stayed in their new lodge, feeling trapped while a guard stood watch outside. They kept brainstorming ways of escape but nothing seemed possible. Hope was beginning to fade.

That night, everyone prayed that God would provide a way of escape.

It was around midnight when Grandpa heard the sound of footsteps entering their lodge.

"Who's there," he asked in a cautious voice.

"It's me." Whispered Watonga. "I've come to help you escape! Wake up everyone, we must hurry."

The children, stretching slowly, woke up thinking they must be dreaming.

"What's going on.?" asked Aria as she rubbed sleep from her eyes.

Watonga explained that he and his father couldn't let them be held captive against their will after all they had done for them. Because they owed them their lives, he would help them escape. Watonga said that the only thing Chief Running Bear demanded is that they must never disclose to anyone the location of the Bear Indians. No one must know the Indians have settled up north in the Barrens.

Grandpa told Watonga, "Tell your father not to worry. We will keep that secrete to our dying days." The children all nodded in agreement.

"My father has given me permission then to help you find where your winter clothes are stashed. Then you can cross the frozen valley. You did have winter clothes when you crossed the valley, didn't you?"

Grandpa answered, "Yes, but we aren't sure where our campsite is where we left them. Our compass that guides us doesn't work in your land."

"Don't worry," Watonga answered. "I will help you find them. I know this land very well."

"Grandpa," asked Maddox. "Am I still dreaming?"

"No," said Grandpa. "Our prayers are being answered. God does make a way when there in none."

"Watonga," asked Taven. "What will happen to you and your father for helping us escape?"

"Our lives will be given for helping you if our tribe finds out. But don't worry, we won't be caught. When they won't find you, they'll think you died trying to escape back across the frozen valley. Watonga then motioned for them to help move a large flat stone that was used as a table on the ground."

The children didn't understand but as they helped slide the heavy stone slab, a tunnel was revealed underneath it.

"This is a secret escape tunnel my grandfather-built years ago just in case we were ever attacked by people crossing over to our land. Fortunately, it was never needed since the frozen valley has always kept people out. That is, until you made it across."

"My father said that this tunnel comes out deep in the woods, away from the village. No one knows this tunnel exists except my father who just told me about it. Your escape will be a mystery to the tribal elders.

"But Watonga,' asked Grandpa. "Won't the elders discover what happened when they see the stone moved and find the tunnel."

"No, my father is coming after we leave to move the stone back in place. After a while, when we are safely out of the tunnel, he will sound the alarm that you are missing. Everything will be OK. No one will know we helped you escape. We owe our lives to you; this is the least we can do.

Watonga unwrapped a heavy deerskin. Inside it were the weapons the bear hunters had used to fight Single Claw. "Hear, you might need these." Instructed Watonga. Quick now, follow me!"

They grabbed their weapons and one by one lowered themselves down into the dark tunnel. The only light was a torch that Watonga held, leading the way. Grandpa was the last to follow, keeping a close watch on the kids. The tunnel wasn't big enough to stand up in and had to be traversed on all fours.

"Wow, this is cool said Maddox."

"Yea, and creepy at the same time." said Aria. "I hope there aren't any spiders down here."

"Don't worry," answered Watonga, "We don't have any spiders or snakes this far north. The cold valley keeps them out."

Everything was going as planned. They had crawled about 200 feet when Watonga stopped.

"What's the matter," asked Aria. "Why are we stopping? Is this the end of the tunnel?"

"I'm not sure." answered Watonga. "Father said this tunnel ran a lot further than this but there's a large tree root blocking us."

Grandpa gave instructions. "Quick Maddox, pass your throwing knives to Watonga so he can cut the root."

Watonga began chopping at the root. "This isn't working." responded Watonga. "The root is way too large and hard. It will take hours to remove it."

Grandpa thought for a moment. "Then we must try to dig to the surface and hope we are far enough away from the village so no one will see us."

Watonga started digging at the ceiling of the tunnel while Aria held the light. Tension was high as everyone waited for Watonga to reach the surface. It was about half an hour before he finally poked through to the outside. Hope was renewed as they began scrambling out of the tunnel. That's when they heard it. War drums! It was the alarm signaling that they had escaped. The pounding of the drums alerted the whole village of their escape. They were supposed to have been far from the village by this time but were only a short distance away because of the plugged tunnel.

"Hurry," said Watonga, "Hide this hole with some brush before we make a run for it. They must not discover this secret tunnel!"

They quickly began grabbing anything they could, leaves, twigs and sticks and covered up the hole in the ground. Then they began running through the dark underbrush putting some distance between them and the village. Fortunately, the Indians began their search inside the village. They went from one lodge to another looking for them. It wasn't until dawn that they began expanding their search into the woods, but they could not find any tracks leading away from the camp. The tunnel had worked as planned after all.

Watonga led them toward the valley of no return.

"This is the general area where you would have crossed over to our land." he said, "but it's not going to be easy to find where you made camp and left your winter parkas. Do you remember anything, like mountains, rivers or trails that would give us a clue?"

Grandpa told Watonga about a small clearing where they camped, not far from a trail along a river they began following when they heard Single Claw.

"The only thing I remember was the large trees and thick underbrush everywhere." said Aria.

"Me too," said Maddox. "All I remember was the huge trees."

"That's it." said Taven, "The trees! Remember what I found stuck up high in one of them. An Indian spear!

Watonga looked surprised. "A spear." he repeated. "Did it have a carving of a bear on it?"

"Yes, it did." answered Taven.

Watonga smiled. "That was my spear. I lost it last year when I was on a hunting trip. I was seeing how far I could throw it when it came down it the trees. I looked and looked but couldn't find it. I know exactly where that spot is."

With renewed hope they followed Watonga through the dark forest.

The sun was beginning to come up by the time they came to the place where Taven had found the spear.

"Yes, this is the trail we were on when we started exploring this land!" exclaimed Grandpa. "We're not far from our camp now."

In no time at all grandpa led them to their tent where their life saving, warm clothes were stashed. The children shouted with joy.

"We're saved!" exclaimed Aria.

Taven and Maddox held hands as they spun in circles.

"We must hurry." said Grandpa. "They'll be time to celebrate later. Put on your parkas and head for the valley. We must cross before we're discovered."

Watonga followed them to where the trail led down to the valley of no return. The thick fog was beginning to envelope them. "How will you find your way across?" asked Watonga. "We've been told the valley is full of trails that you would get lost in."

Grandpa kept looking down at the ground and then bent over and picked up a string. "You see this. I tied this string to the main trail when it began to branch off into many little trails. All we have to do is follow it and it will lead us back across.

"That was wise of you." said Watonga. "Now my spirit won't have to worry."

They all turned to Watonga to say their goodbyes.

"We will never forget what you and your father did for us." said Grandpa.

"Nor I for you." said Watonga. "I will always keep you in my memory."

After a group hug, Grandpa and the Bear Hunters disappeared into the fog as they started back across the frozen death trap. In no time at all they came out on the other side, into their own world. Watonga headed back to his village where someday, he would become chief.

"I wonder if we'll ever see Watonga again?" asked Maddox.

"I doubt it." answered Grandpa. "But I left the string on the ground just in case he ever wanted, or needed, to come over to where we live. Don't forget, we must keep the discovery of the Bear Indians to ourselves." The children all nodded in agreement.

Their return trip went smoothly with no encounters with Single Claw. After several days, they came down the hill where they could see Sawdust Springs. Their hearts were filled with a joy they will treasure forever.

Grandma came out of the log cabin to greet them. "Well, it's sure good to have you back safe and sound. This is probably the first time you made it back when you said you would. Guess it must have been a boring trip?"

The children just looked at each other and smiled.

www.ingramcontent.com/pod-product-compliance
Ingram Content Group UK Ltd.
Pitfield, Milton Keynes, MK11 3LW, UK
UKHW032333131224
452011UK00004B/45

9 798868 505423